After a day exploring the wonders of the Roman Empire, do as the Romans did and head for the baths!

Come up to the Helios deck and relax your tired muscles in one of the Jasmine Spa's petal-strewn baths. It's the perfect way to prepare for the night's activities aboard ship. Soak in the outdoor bath with a panoramic view of the azure sea, or enjoy the calm and quiet of the indoor bath. The towering Roman pillars will transport you back to the ancient days of the empire.

Highly trained spa therapists offer you a range of services from hot stone massages to seaweed wraps. Feel the tension of modern life disappear from body and soul as you surrender to the age-old rhythms of the Mediterranean. *Alexandra's Dream* offers you the best of both worlds—ancient treatments in ultramodern comfort. Book early and discover the three R's of cruising. The Jasmine Spa will help you relax and rejuvenate. The romance is up to you!

DORIEN KELLY

is a former attorney who is much happier as an author. In addition to her years practicing business law, at one point or another she has also been a waitress, a bank teller, a law-school teaching assistant and a professional chauffeur to her three children.

When Dorien isn't writing, she loves to garden, travel and avoid doing the laundry. A RITA® Award nominee, she is also the winner of the Romance Writers of America's Golden Heart Award, a Booksellers' Best Award, a Maggie Award, an Aspen Gold Award and a Gayle Wilson Award of Excellence. She lives in a small village in Michigan with her children and three crazed dogs.

Mediterranean NIGHTS™

Dorien Kelly

BELOW DECK

HARLEQUIN®

TORONTO • NEW YORK • LONDON
AMSTERDAM • PARIS • SYDNEY • HAMBURG
STOCKHOLM • ATHENS • TOKYO • MILAN • MADRID
PRAGUE • WARSAW • BUDAPEST • AUCKLAND

ISBN-13: 978-0-373-38965-0
ISBN-10:   0-373-38965-5

BELOW DECK

Copyright © 2007 by Harlequin Books S.A.

Dorien Kelly is acknowledged as the author of this work.

This edition published by arrangement with Harlequin Books S.A.

® and TM are trademarks of the publisher. Trademarks indicated with ® are registered in the United States Patent and Trademark Office, the Canadian Trade Marks Office and in other countries.

www.eHarlequin.com

Printed in U.S.A.

Dear Reader,

Real life and fiction writing have an odd way of taking the same path. For me, this past year has been one filled with changes—some wonderful, some more difficult...and many quite out of my control.

In the same way, my heroine, Mei Lin Wang, has been forced by circumstances to grapple with destiny, danger and loss. Lin is about to learn that she is stronger than she thinks...perhaps strong enough to embrace that most challenging gift of all—love!

I hope you enjoy my contribution to Harlequin's MEDITERRANEAN NIGHTS series of novels. I love to hear from my readers! Visit my Web site at www.dorienkelly.com or e-mail me at dorien@dorienkelly.com.

Wishing you all the best!

Dorien Kelly

It has been one wild year. My love and gratitude to many resilient, wonderful women: Caitlin Kelly, Erin Kelly, Sean O'Tuathal, Mary Schumaker, Kathy Burch, Carole Burch, Gail Blackburn, Kathy Crawford, Joan Smith, Jennifer Green, those who know about the Alamo, and my loopers. That which does not kill us makes us smarter, stronger and more determined!

DON'T MISS THE STORIES OF

Mediterranean
NIGHTS™

FROM RUSSIA, WITH LOVE
Ingrid Weaver

SCENT OF A WOMAN
Joanne Rock

THE TYCOON'S SON
Cindy Kirk

BREAKING ALL THE RULES
Marisa Carroll

AN AFFAIR TO REMEMBER
Karen Kendall

BELOW DECK
Dorien Kelly

A PERFECT MARRIAGE?
Cindi Myers

FULL EXPOSURE
Diana Duncan

CABIN FEVER
Mary Leo

ISLAND HEAT
Sarah Mayberry

STARSTRUCK
Michelle Celmer

THE WAY HE MOVES
Marcia King-Gamble

CHAPTER ONE

Often one finds one's destiny just where one
hides to avoid it.

—*Chinese Proverb*

SLEEP. To Mei Lin Wang, the word was paradise, a
prize more valued than the tiny staff cabin on *Alexandra's Dream* that she'd had nearly to herself since the
cruise ship's other massage therapist had fallen ill and
returned home.

Sleep. She would never have enough of it.
Someday when silver ran thick through her hair and
she was free to do as she wished, she would nap in
the sun, laze in the shade and rest while the moonlight
washed over her.

Not this late September morning, though.

"Hush, my little warrior," she murmured in her native
tongue to her son, Wei, who fussed in the reed basket
that served as both his crib and a secretive means of
transport about the ship. Though he was nearly five
months old and healthy, Wei remained small. Lin
knew from poring over articles on the computer in the
ship's Internet café that since he was breast-fed, she

shouldn't be concerned, but she was a mother, and worry was as common in her life as sleep was rare.

Before lifting Wei from his basket, Lin glanced at her bedside clock, though she needn't have. Wei was his late father's son, down to his determined approach to the day. It was, as she knew it would be, 5:00 a.m., and her child demanded feeding.

This was her favorite time of the morning, when the ship's corridors were relatively quiet, and the press of the day hadn't begun to consume her. Wei snuggled at her breast, his small hand settled against her as he nursed. Five perfect little fingers on one supremely perfect hand... All would be well as he grew; she would have it no other way.

As her child greedily fed, Lin permitted herself to truly relax. Her eyes slipped closed, and she sighed as she considered just how far she'd traveled. Small wonder she was weary. Five years ago, she had been in the chill of her home city of Harbin, yearning to test her English teaching skills in Beijing. Five hundred days ago, she'd been in that capital city, a secret wife to baby Wei's father. Five months ago, she'd been large and ungainly with child, fighting to hold on to her job as a massage therapist at a posh Hong Kong hotel.

And now, though *Alexandra's Dream* was not her final stopping point, it sheltered her well. She had money of her own, certainly not enough to be considered wealthy, but nearly enough to fund the start of a new life with compatriots in Paris. It had been a gamble, sneaking Wei aboard. But for her longtime Beijing friend, Zhang, who was in charge of the ship's laundry, she would not have risked it. Even now, over three months later, she knew the danger of being discovered grew daily.

But as the secret wife—then widow—of Wei Chan, a human rights activist as revered by some as he'd been reviled by others, she was no stranger to risk and danger. They had been her constant companions these past three years. If she were to evade the Chinese authorities whispered to be seeking her, and seize her destiny as she intended, those same companions would be with her until she reached the end of her life.

"Grow strong," she whispered to her son as she switched him from one breast to the other. They would have to be strong to face what was to come....

Once Wei was fed, rediapered and dressed for the day, Lin hurriedly swigged from a bottle of water, as nursing always left her thirsty, then turned her attention to her own simple preparations: a quick shower, dressing in her plain spa uniform of white polo top and slim-fitting white pants. Wei, with his beloved pacifier in his mouth, contentedly watched from his basket. Finally, Lin knotted her hair into a thick twist at the back of her head.

She shook her head at her reflection in the small mirror over her sink. A sleek bob would be simpler to handle, more modern, too, but her hair was her sole vanity. Wei Chan had once said that if he were to die, he'd wish to drown in her hair. She'd chided him for the dark thought, then made love to him until they'd both been breathless and felt indisputably alive. Sometimes she woke at night and still reached for him, but he was gone—had been for the past year—lost to her forever. And though her heart still ached, each day she grew a little stronger, just as she'd instructed baby Wei to do. Each day she learned to live for her son and her future.

A soft knock sounded at the door—one rap, silence, then two more raps—her code with Zhang. Lin admitted her friend.

"You eat first this morning. You look as though you need it more than I," Zhang said.

Lin smiled at the comment, for petite Zhang reminded her of a dark, exotic hummingbird, always flitting about and always in need of food. Lin thought herself of sturdier stock, arms and hands strong from her work, and feet solid on the ground from hours spent standing. If she were a bird, she'd be more like a pelican, storing her strength for the future.

"I'll go first only because it will save me the time I could spend arguing with you," Lin replied.

Zhang gave a brisk nod of her head, then settled on the bed next to Wei's basket. "Our little warrior looks content today."

"As he should be," Lin said. "With his every need tended to."

"And now you must tend to yours," Zhang directed.

True to her word, Lin made her way to the crew dining room, where, as on every other morning, breakfast was served. But unlike other mornings, a cluster of people stood waiting for seats in the room. She looked about impatiently. One empty chair wasn't so much to ask, was it?

Apparently so. Her stomach rumbled, and her mouth felt as dry and parched as an old woman's.

"We all had the same idea...an early start," said Dima Ivanov, a staff member in the ship's fitness center, who waited in line before her.

She had danced a few times with Dima during her one venture to a nightclub in Corsica several weeks ago. Since then, he always seemed to be wherever she was. She knew that this was not simply because his place of work was adjacent to hers. Though on one level she was flattered by his attention, she was not attracted to him. And even if she were, she could hardly afford to bring someone into her life. Too many knew about her child as it was.

"It does seem we're all on the same schedule," she replied, her voice ringing oddly in her ears.

She closed her eyes, exhaled, and fought to bring herself back into the moment. The room seemed to grow smaller. Languages swirled around her: Greek, Swedish, English...

"Are you feeling all right?" Dima asked.

"I'm not sure. Just tired, I think."

"Let me find you a seat," he offered.

Lin shook her head. "Not just now."

She had to get out before the room swallowed her whole. She slipped into the hallway and dragged in a deep breath. Fireworks danced in front of her eyes...glittering silver-gold chrysanthemums. Quite beautiful, she was sure. Except that she also felt cold and ill and thirsty enough that she leaned back against the wall and slid slowly to the floor. She brought one shaking hand to her forehead, which was unnaturally cool and dappled with perspiration.

Had she the strength, she would have smiled at the irony of her situation. Her early-morning wish was being visited upon her. She'd craved sleep, and now, when the day's duties awaited her, she was to receive that...or something darker. Unbidden and now unwanted, but indisputably hers...

COMFORT. REST. NIGHT. A warm yet slightly rough hand settled against the side of her face, and a set of fingertips rested at her throat. The clean, honest scent of soap and perhaps a whisper of sandalwood wafted over her. Another dream, it had to be. Lin embraced it.

Wei, my love.

The hand that had been at her face settled more firmly against her upper arm, its grip authoritative, yet not unpleasant.

"Miss Wang?"

She frowned, for the speaker used English, and his accent was distinctly un-Chinese. The hand shook her arm insistently, forcing her to rouse the rest of the way to consciousness.

She opened her eyes and focused on the man's face so close to hers. It was rugged, with a bold nose broken at least once in its owner's life.

"You fainted," he said.

Lin managed a nod.

He held a glass to her lips. "Drink."

A command, but this came as no surprise since Gideon Dayan was doing the speaking. The ship's chief security officer was a man of few words, and all of them firm.

Because she disliked showing weakness to any man, especially one so certain of his own strength, Lin sat more firmly upright and took the water from him. She swallowed it quickly and felt her world begin to right itself. She realized then that a small crowd had gathered behind Officer Dayan.

Following her line of vision, he looked over his shoulder. "That will be all," he said to the group.

They dispersed—even devoted Dima—sending a few "glad you're okays" and "feel betters" Lin's way. For her part, she would have preferred that Dima or virtually anyone else among the spectators had stayed, and Gideon Dayan had been on his way. He was the last soul on this ship she needed noticing her. Beyond that, he made her uncomfortable on some other level she'd much rather not consider, so she avoided him whenever possible. He had come to her for her services as a massage therapist, and on each of those occasions she'd been too aware of him…too uncomfortable, as she was now.

"I've paged for medical assistance," he said.

To wait for the doctor to confirm that she'd merely fainted, when Zhang waited for her with Wei?

Impossible. Any delay in their morning ritual would mean that Zhang would miss her opportunity to eat.

"That won't be necessary," she replied. "I'm much better now." She thrust the glass back at him, then worked her way to her feet.

She wondered if she looked as much like an awkwardly scrabbling crab as she felt. And then she wondered why she cared whether she showed any grace in front of this man. No matter. The time had come to flee.

His broad hand closed over her arm once again. What had been pleasant in her half-aware state was now startling. His touch made her think of just how long it had been since someone other than herself had initiated the touching. It also made her feel too open, when she'd grown to like her closed-off life.

Lin glanced up at his face, some six inches above her own. She fancied she saw a glimmer of the same sort of unwilling awareness in his gray eyes. But, no. As soon as the thought came to her, his face was as impassive as it always seemed. She subtly drew her arm away and made a step to skirt around him.

"Thank you for your help, but—"

He blocked her way. "The call to the doctor remains outstanding and will continue that way unless you let me see you to the medical centre."

"I have no time. I'm due in the spa in minutes." Alarm had crept into her voice. Again, she mentally chided herself for showing weakness. Lin drew in a breath and calmed. "As you can see, I am well."

His gaze traveled down the length of her body.

"I can see that you're fit, but I have no way of

knowing that you are well," he replied, his voice level and measured. "And I have also been told by Dima Ivanov that you have yet to eat."

"Perhaps I ate before I saw Dima."

"And perhaps not. I'll cancel the medical page if you come with me into the officers' dining room, where I can personally be sure that you have breakfast."

"I am not a child, needing watching."

"I'm aware of that, Miss Wang," he said. Once more that glint of something—humor, maybe—danced in his eyes just briefly enough that Lin doubted she'd seen it at all.

"I'll take an orange or an apple," she said. "Whatever can be found that I can eat on my way to my duties."

"Your devotion to your job is admirable, but you'll do neither yourself nor the passengers any good if you work when you're ill."

"I am not ill!" How she wished that she could blurt the truth—that she'd been careless and had not drunk enough fluids to nurse Wei without becoming faint. "I...I forgot to eat dinner last night and I'm overhungry." It was a lie, since she'd eaten the chef's pasta with Greek olives and artichoke hearts like a piglet, but it wasn't a lie that this man could catch her in.

"If you insist," he said, then drew her into the crew's dining room, where two of the waitresses nearly raced to see who could reach him first.

"Could you please bring Miss Wang some fruit and perhaps a muffin or other pastry?" he asked.

The winner of the race nodded enthusiastically. "Anything else, sir?"

"Anything?" he asked Lin.

"Nothing," she replied.

"Bottled juice, too, if you can find some," he said instead to the waitress.

"Yes, sir." She shot toward the service door as though her future relied upon getting the requested items.

"Do you always receive this sort of response?" Lin asked the man she refused to think of as her rescuer.

His mouth quirked into a slightly crooked smile, one that remained long enough for her to accept as real.

"Definitely not," he said, and she realized he was referring to her blatantly unreceptive attitude.

"Then better to stay with those who appreciate you," she said, thinking that since he seemed the humorless sort, her dry comment might repel him.

Instead, he laughed. "But far less entertaining."

She had not measured her opponent properly. Sparking any interest at all was dangerous. It was far better that she be as bland as the sturdy blue carpet beneath their feet.

"I promise you I'll take my food to the spa and eat between appointments, sir," she offered in as meek a voice as she knew how to summon. "And I thank you for taking time from your morning to help me."

Ah, that seemed to have worked.

The chief security officer briefly frowned, then inclined his head in a nod. "As you wish, Miss Wang." He moved two steps toward the door and then turned back. "Take care of yourself."

After he was gone, Lin wondered why it was that those simple words sounded like a warning? She would take care, indeed.

GIDEON DAYAN would have once said that he prided himself on knowing the name and face of every Liberty Line employee on *Alexandra's Dream*. But that arrogant, if accurate, boast would only have been spoken in the "before" part of his life…before he'd learned the lesson that pride had the potential to be fatal. Now that he bore the marks of that lesson, he was quietly thankful for the military and academic training that had honed his abilities and kept him alive in spite of foolish arrogance. And, as he'd discovered earlier this morning, he now seemed to be more alive than he'd thought himself in some time.

Leaning back in his office chair, he used his computer's mouse to page through the daily safety and security updates that, as Chief of Security and Surveillance, he received from sources as diverse as Interpol, the International Maritime Organization and his own employer's home office staff. As there was little news, he considered instead his breakfast encounter with Mei Lin Wang.

He wasn't quite sure how a woman so stunning in person could appear to be so unremarkable on paper, but she'd achieved just that. He knew from personal experience that she was a skilled masseuse, polite and thorough. From what he'd gleaned from her personnel file, she'd been born in Harbin, college educated in

Harbin and Beijing and trained as a massage therapist at a well-respected school in Hong Kong. Her references, impeccable. Demeanor, respectful at all times.

More accurately, nearly at all times. Gideon smiled as he recalled the way she'd bristled at him, as though accepting his help was tantamount to failure. Leaving her a measure of her dignity had been the right thing to do, even though he'd felt an odd impulse to stay and protect her. Odd both because his help had been unappreciated, and because it had been a very long time since he'd felt anything other than a distant sort of interest in a woman. But while Lin intrigued him, she was not Rachel.

Gideon rubbed absently at the scarred and always aching flesh that ran the length of his right thigh and knotted into his knee. That scar—and the others his body bore—were the physical reminders of Rachel. But other reminders ran deeper—a dark river through his psyche. And as he did each time she whispered to him, Gideon directed his focus to the here and now.

The four months he'd spent recuperating—first in the hospital and then in his Tel Aviv apartment—immediately following the incident that changed his life had been enough to drive him mad. He required action to keep his mind sharp, which was why he'd asked his superiors at Israel's secret service, the Mossad, for permission to take this job while on indefinite leave. But before winter came to the Mediterranean, his contracted time with the cruise line would draw to a close.

On some days he hungered to rush home and resume

his regular duties. Just as frequently, he asked himself if he wasn't ready for the relatively bloodless world of corporate security. Many questions, countless hours spent weighing the options, but as of yet, no answers. Luckily, he had much to distract him in his last weeks of temporary employment.

Even a ship as smoothly run as *Alexandra's Dream* had its share of security issues. In the past few months, on top of the usual passenger disputes and other standard fare, he'd had to deal with a small find of stolen antiquities, a Russian hired killer, an abusive husband out for revenge and the recent, odd departure of the ship's librarian, Ariana Bennett, who hadn't returned to the ship in Naples. Beyond that, there were more than a few crew and staff members that Gideon remained convinced were not as fine and upstanding as they claimed to be…Miss Wang included.

The crew was growing tense, and rumors abounded. To compound matters, they had just left yesterday evening from Istanbul, Turkey, on two fully booked seven-day, back-to-back cruises, which meant no respite for the crew, and an endless stream of new faces aboard ship. Gideon had no doubt that his days would be full.

He scanned his command center's bank of small video screens with their black-and-white views of the ship's public areas, and spotted Sean Brady, his next in command on the security team, talking with another of the ship's staff, Father Connelly, in the casino.

"No surprise," he said to himself, though it would

have been even less a surprise if he'd seen the ship's first officer, Giorgio Tzekas, who was known to have a gambling problem.

All the same, the sight of Connelly in the casino so early in the day was exactly the reason he'd quietly asked Sean to keep an eye on the man. Gideon had never noted Connelly, an academic hired as a lecturer on the antiquities, doing anything precisely wrong, and, like Miss Wang, on paper Father Connelly raised no alarms. Still, gut instinct told him that—priest or not— the man bore watching.

The same instinct told Gideon that Lin Wang was trying too hard to blend into the background. Those who said one thing while their body language shouted another needed to be watched. At least, that's what he preferred to think sparked his interest in her.

His small two-way radio, a constant companion, buzzed. Gideon pulled it from its holster and flipped it open.

"Dayan," he answered.

"That's one damn chatty priest," Sean Brady said. "Are you sure I can't hand him off to someone else to watch?"

"No, he's yours. I don't want to entrust him to anyone else."

"So this is my punishment for being trusted? Did I ever mention that I spent all of my formative years in Catholic schools?"

"No, but all the more reason you're the ideal man for the job."

"Yeah, and all the more reason I need a break," Brady groused.

Gideon glanced at the monitor. Connelly was surrounded by a ring of elderly, admiring women, and Brady was no longer in the camera's view. "It appears you're getting a break now."

"Lucky me. You're going to owe me for this, and I don't mean just a thanks and a note in my employment file.... I mean more like one helluva night out the next time we get off this ship together."

Brady had become more than a highly valued subordinate over the past several months. The square-jawed, tough, former U.S. Army Green Beret was someone Gideon counted among his true friends...one of the few people aboard ship he fully trusted, even if he chose to keep certain personal doors closed to the man.

"I want you on Connelly's tail tomorrow in Kusadasi," Gideon said. "I want to know what he does when he's not under our cameras."

"I can answer that already. He talks. That's all he does."

"Then he's not much of a listener for a man supposedly trained to give counsel, is he?"

"Point grudgingly taken," Brady said. "You're right to have me watching the guy."

"As you'd say, Brady, I'm batting one thousand," Gideon replied, then flipped shut his radio.

Gideon pushed away from his desk and readied to begin his midmorning walk of the ship. He, too, would stop and chat with the priest because he was nothing if not a thorough man. And for the same reason his rounds would include a stop at the spa and a visit with Lin Wang.

He smiled at the thought of seeing the masseuse again. Sometimes the payoff for being thorough was nothing short of rich....

CHAPTER TWO

LIN'S HANDS ACHED and her shoulders cried for a rest. What she wouldn't give for a massage, except, of course, she was the sole massage therapist left in the Jasmine Spa, and thus the reason for her woes. At least part of her woes. Her aching breasts were no fault but her own for trying to hide poor Wei as though he were a package to be delivered from place to place instead of the child of her heart and soul.

She needed to call Zhang and see if her friend could slip Wei into the calm of the private massage room for a quick feeding, since Lin had no time to make it to Zhang's small closet of an office on the perimeter of the ship's laundry. A guest had booked a last-minute massage through the spa's receptionist, despite the fact that Lin had blocked out a thirty-minute break for herself, and she had been unable to tell Zhang of the change.

Lingering in the spa's entry, Lin glanced longingly at the receptionist's phone and with less enthusiasm at Helga, the dragon who guarded it. It seemed the woman never left her desk, not even for a quick trip to the restroom. Lin often wondered if the receptionist were actually human.

"We have twenty minutes before my next client," Lin said. "I'd be happy to watch the phone for you if you'd like a break."

"I am needed here," Helga replied, placing the palms of her broad hands on the mahogany reception desk. Just then the phone rang, as though to back up her territorial assertion. Helga gave Lin a dismissive nod, then answered it.

Lin walked back through the archway that led to the first of the ship's two small Roman baths that were the centerpiece of the spa. This one looked out a bank of windows at the vista of an endless blue sea and today's equally limitless blue sky.

The Mediterranean weather was perfect for cruising, and the few women lounging in the pool seemed to relish the perfection of the moment, too. Lin nodded a friendly hello to the guests. She then moved on to the dimmer, meditative light of the Jasmine pool, with its scattering of white Jasmine petals richly perfuming the air, and then finally into the serenity of her small massage room, just off the pool.

If she could not call Zhang and Wei to her by conventional means, she could at least wish them here. Lin riffled through the collection of music on compact discs that she kept for those clients who wished something other than silence while using her services. Most of the music was the ambient sort...no words, nothing to distract...just soothing tunes. She selected her favorite, then settled in the plump blue velvet chair that was for the guests' comfort as they changed into their clothes, but which also was the perfect size in which to nurse a baby.

Sleep still called to her. She let her eyes slip shut as she thought of her sweet boy, with his wild shock of fine black hair. Moments later, a soft series of raps sounded at the door—not Helga's firmer announcement that a client awaited, but Zhang's code.

Lin rose and opened the door.

"Your fresh towels," Zhang offered, holding out the large and sturdy reed basket with its white linen draping off the arched center handle, hiding a cargo far more precious than towels.

Lin glanced behind her friend to be sure that Helga wasn't lurking in the shadows. It seemed that the dragon was at her desk.

"We're alone," Zhang said in their shared language of Huayu, the universal form of Chinese used at university, and most certainly unintelligible to ninety-nine percent of those aboard *Alexandra's Dream*. "And we need to speak."

Lin ushered her into the massage room and closed the door after her. She wasted no time in taking Wei from his basket and getting him to her overfull breast. While she settled in, Zhang propped herself on the edge of the massage table.

She must have caught Lin's concerned frown because she said, "I'll bring more clean sheets if it's the laundry you're worried about. I'm certainly here enough during the day."

Lin sighed. "As much as you're here, it's not enough

to keep Wei satisfied and still too much to assure our safety. I hate risking your job like this."

"It's my risk and my choice. Besides, if you're worried about Helga, relax." Zhang gave a casual shrug of her shoulders. "I'm sure she just assumes that we're in here shirking our duties. She always looks as though she's tasted something horribly sour when I say hello."

"How can you be so calm? We've come too close to being caught too many times."

Zhang smiled. "Ah, but you're missing the best part. We *haven't* been caught, and it's more than luck that has it this way. Young Wei's father is watching over us. He's exactly the sort to impose his will even when reduced to a spirit."

Zhang would know. Besides having been a classmate in Beijing, she was also a cousin to Lin's late husband, and had been active in his efforts to bring economic and social freedoms and equality to their people. Zhang had been so active that a hasty escape from her opposition's reach had been necessary. *Alexandra's Dream* had become her home...one she now loved. For reasons of family bond as well as her own wishes to see the elder Wei's work continued, Zhang had suggested this means of getting Lin and baby Wei the funds to safely move from the dangers of home to Paris. Luckily, Zhang's network of friends aboard ship were as close and close-lipped as those they had shared in Beijing.

"Let's hope Wei keeps up his determination for another two weeks," Lin said. She was due to leave the ship when it returned to Piraeus after the current back-to-back cruises.

"That's nothing for the son of Wei Chan," Zhang replied. "Did I ever tell you of the time Wei Chan challenged my brother to a contest to see who could hold his breath the longest? Both the fools nearly fainted." She chuckled. "I thought my mother was going to faint, too. The more she chided them, the longer they held on."

"And that's what I've been doing these last days…holding my breath. I have…" Lin dug for the words to explain the uncomfortable feeling that had settled in her bones. "I have…I don't know…just the sense that everything is about to change."

"Change is inevitable…and good," Zhang replied.

"Not all change is good," Lin said as she switched hungry Wei from her left breast to her right. Losing Wei Chan had been far from good. She had seen her heart and life shattered. If not for her very new pregnancy, she might have swallowed her anger and quietly slipped home to Harbin. But her baby—Wei Chan's baby—had reminded her that Wei's goals could be reached for the son, if not the father. Also she had discovered that fury could be a fine motivator, and so she had made her plans to step in where her child's father had left off.

Zhang moved from the edge of the massage table to the small cart where Lin kept her massage supplies. She opened a vial of lavender essential oil and dabbed some on the insides of her wrists. As the oil's scent wafted to Lin, she let its relaxing qualities ease her troubled mind.

"Change is as good as you make it," Zhang said. "And I have faith that you will make it good, or I wouldn't have urged you to take this job. Think about this. Few people know of your marriage to Wei Chan, and even fewer of your child's existence. Not your parents, not Wei Chan's...no one. You could not have been more careful. If something were to have gone wrong, it would have been when you obtained Wei's passport or when you came aboard ship."

Lin was about to reply when a sharp rap sounded at the door—one made by a dragon's claw. Though she'd started at the sound, Lin kept her voice level as she called to Helga through the closed door.

"Yes?"

"You are needed at the desk."

"I'll be there in a moment," she said in a voice loud enough to carry to the receptionist. In a softer tone, she added to Zhang, "My appointment must be here early. Now I'll be lopsided and Wei will be grumpy until lunchtime. Where shall we meet?"

"Your cabin," Zhang said as she prepared Wei's basket. "I can't believe that we don't have even one empty stateroom on this ship."

They'd worked out a system of using empty staterooms and the master passkey Zhang had as part of her job to aid in their hiding of baby Wei, but had hit a snag on this busy cruise. Lin removed Wei from her breast and snuggled him close.

"That's my little warrior," she whispered to him when he kept his protests to a small, angry grunt.

Zhang took the baby from her. Lin stood and quickly restored her clothing, again tucking her shirt into her white pants. Since she could catch the sweet scents of milk and baby on her skin, she quickly dabbed some lavender oil on herself, too. One could never be too careful.

She opened the door, expecting to see the dragon, but the woman had moved on, thank the heavens.

"Noon exactly…my cabin," she said quietly to Zhang, then slipped out, leaving her friend to exit when the hallway was empty and the time right.

Lin took more time than usual walking the short distance to the spa's entry. All the better to let Helga settle and give Zhang time to depart. Her steps slowed even more when she saw who awaited her—not a passenger desiring a little pampering, but Gideon Dayan. She had no words for him, so she nodded in greeting, then focused on Helga.

"My ten o'clock appointment?" she asked the receptionist.

"Would be here eleven minutes early," replied the woman, looking at her watch.

Helga was nothing if not precise. Lin drew in a slow breath and made sure that she had a pleasant expression in place. "Then why am I needed up here?"

"I had asked if you might fit me in for a massage," Gideon said. "Helga said that you had a possible opening, but that she couldn't call you in your room because your phone seems to be broken."

"She kept disconnecting it until it couldn't be fixed," the receptionist very unhelpfully informed Gideon.

"To disable equipment is a violation of ship rules, as I'm sure you know, Miss Wang," he said.

Ah, how she had hoped that she would not be compelled to engage with this man. Even without being goaded, Lin found it difficult to remain calm in his presence. He was not the most attractive man she had ever seen. On the contrary, with the hint of a frown that often seemed to linger between his brows, some might think him plain. Yet her contrary heart stumbled when she was close to him.

"The phone disturbs my clients," Lin replied. "Until recently, I was able to plug it back in when I needed it…a simple task."

"Even if it were working, it's not so easy to finish a simple task if you're cornered," the security officer replied.

"I don't corner easily." Her words didn't carry much weight, since for the second time in the same morning, Gideon Dayan had done just that.

"Then you're versed in Kung Fu?" he asked, easing himself even closer to her. "Perhaps a follower of the forms of the legendary Ng Mui?"

Again, her heart stumbled. Few aboard ship appeared to know or care very much about her culture, let alone this sort of detail. When Lin had been a girl, her mother had often told her tales of bold Ng Mui, a Buddhist nun who had lived centuries ago, creating her own form of the esteemed martial art and supposedly saving a temple with her skills.

"I lacked the discipline to advance," Lin replied to Gideon.

"Doubtful," Gideon said. "You've accomplished too much for that to be true."

It came as no surprise that he would have read her file. Still, she chafed at his advantage over her.

"Please call to have Ms. Wang's phone repaired," the officer directed Helga, who had been avidly watching their exchange.

Lin knew that she'd be the subject of lunchtime gossip in the dining room. The ship's crew and staff were no different than a small village, with rumors being vividly embellished. She doubted that her run-in with Gideon would be enough to permanently supplant the current topic of her friend Ariana Bennett's disappearance. Still, after seeing Helga's smirk, she knew that word would pass from table to table, all the same. She shot the annoying dragon a look with more than a little fire in it.

"Lin is free at noon," the receptionist told Gideon in a clear case of retaliation.

"I always take my lunch at noon," Lin said. More accurately, she took her lunch at noon unless Helga scheduled her in with more appointments despite Lin's strict instructions that that sole hour remain free.

"Fifteen minutes is all I need," Gideon said. "I'll even see that lunch is delivered to you."

"Noon," the receptionist repeated. She had already begun entering Gideon's appointment into the computer's scheduling program.

"I'm afraid the answer must remain no, though I appreciate your continuing efforts to fatten me," Lin said aloud, mentally adding, *like a hapless goose being readied for the kill.* She briefly ducked her head to hide her smile, but not before she'd noted the surprised looks from both the dragon and Dayan.

"If not at noon, then at the end of your day?" he suggested.

She knew she could push no further to escape without becoming more firmly trapped in this man's attention.

"Eight-thirty, then," she said.

She was about to turn away when his hand settled briefly on her shoulder.

"And do keep the phone connected, Miss Wang," he said.

Lin hid the shiver of awareness passing though her by shrugging away from his touch.

"Of course, sir," she replied, then brushed by him as quickly as she could. Sometimes, the wisest thing a woman could do was retreat.

GIDEON KNEW THAT in a clinical sense he wasn't claustrophobic. All the same, the ship's confines seemed to be growing smaller with each passing day. When he'd first come aboard *Alexandra's Dream,* his office had been his sanctuary. He'd spent most of his day in front of his bank of monitors, watching all from afar. Of course, walking hadn't been one of his favorite activities at that point. The wounds he'd sustained had torn muscle once strong and destroyed enough of his knee that he'd been told that walking at all would be a miracle.

Gideon didn't believe in miracles. Certainly none had touched him. Walking as well as he did was the product of pain and struggle and hours spent with relentless physical therapists. Aboard ship, he'd continued his regime, favoring the hours when the gym was empty, leaving him no need to keep up a facade of invulnerability. From there, he'd branched out to his current routine. Unless giving or attending a briefing, or making sure that the monitors were covered, he walked. By now, he could identify each hallway of each deck by the pattern of its floor covering, and each wall by any slight scratches it might hold. All that ever changed were the passengers, and to some smaller degree, the ports.

Tomorrow's stop in Kusadasi was one that Gideon planned to take advantage of. The busy Turkish tourist port could prove to be just the distraction he required. While the ship's passengers did their sightseeing, he would walk the city to clear his mind of the ship's passageways and of Lin Wang.

As he strode through the hotel's main reception area, where clusters of passengers waited patiently to book shore excursions or chat with one of the ship's concierge staff, he wondered whether Lin's hair would fall sleek and straight if it ever escaped from the severe knot she favored. The color was as dark as Rachel's, but the texture appeared to be different. His fingers twitched as he imagined touching that hair, freeing it from its twist, and then…

He shook his head at his insanity. *And then what?* It

had been a big enough mistake to touch her shoulder. Better to recall that he was leaving, that he wasn't the sort to seduce or be seduced into a quick and meaningless fling, and that Mei Lin Wang didn't appear to be the sort to fall into seduction, in any case. Along with his walk tomorrow, he'd have a few glasses of acrid *raki*, the local drink of choice. That should be enough to shake loose Miss Wang.

"Officer Dayan…sir…Gideon…hey! Gideon?"

Gideon looked back over his shoulder. Sean Brady was closing in on him.

"I've been on your tail since you got off the elevator. Didn't you hear me call you?"

"Sorry," Gideon said. "Just thinking through some things."

"Like what, global warming or world peace?"

"Just about as complex," Gideon replied.

Brady grinned, and from a purely objective point of view, Gideon could see why the younger man had such a following among the women.

"Interesting…" Brady said. "If it were anyone but you, I'd say you were referring to a woman, but for all that they come on to you, I've never seen you so much as look at one."

Sean Brady might be a friend, but Gideon kept certain parts of his life off-limits. No one other than the ship's captain, Nick Pappas, knew of his past, and that was only because Gideon fully believed in reporting all germane details to a direct superior.

"Do you have something to report?" Gideon asked,

tacitly reminding Sean that duty came before everything else.

Sean's smile faded, and once again he was all business.

"Father Connelly is going to be taking a group of passengers on a morning lecture tour of the ruins at Ephesus. I'll be going with the group."

"Good," Gideon replied.

"I'll chat him up…see if I can get him to give out a little more personal history, one good Catholic boy to another. I'm sure he's crossed paths with a Jesuit teacher or two of mine."

Gideon nodded, then checked his watch. He was nearly due for his daily briefing with Captain Pappas. "Get your notes into Father Connelly's file as soon as possible, and then start looking for discrepancies."

Brady smiled again, though this smile had a hunter's predatory edge to it. "If there's one to be found, it's mine."

Gideon didn't doubt that for a second.

Minutes later, he was on the bridge, awaiting his daily audience with Nick Pappas. Gideon respected the ship's master for his skill and focus, but also because the captain had been willing to give him this place of refuge. Not many would accept a man as emotionally raw as Gideon had been upon hire. Not many, except Nick Pappas. Back when Gideon was hired, Nick had been more staid, more regimented than he was now, which had made his decision to hire Gideon all the more startling.

Even now, the Greek captain was as closemouthed about personal matters as Gideon, and still a strict follower of formality while on the bridge. But Gideon knew what Nick had been through in the past few weeks. Gideon had been there just after Nick had freed himself and Helena Stamos, daughter of the ship's owner, from an attacker. He had seen the sort of love the now-engaged couple had shared. As far as Gideon was concerned, true love was rarer than those ever-absent miracles in life, and he was happy for both Nick and Helena.

"Anything new?" the captain asked, while simultaneously paging though a file that another officer had handed him.

"Nothing out of the ordinary, sir. We have a handful of passengers that the home office has flagged for prior incidents, one family dispute last night and a few more comments from the crew about Ariana Bennett. I assured them yet again that all procedures were followed regarding Miss Bennett, and that if there is evidence of anything other than a willing departure from her job, the Italian authorities will follow up on it."

The captain gave Gideon his full attention. "Do *you* have any growing concerns regarding Miss Bennett?"

Gideon considered his answer carefully. Between the find of that small antiquities cache hidden in a potted plant, and the fact that a little research had disclosed that Ariana Bennett's father had been charged with dealing in illegal antiquities, the possible connection niggled at him. And then there was the matter of the way her name had become linked with that of First Officer Giorgio Tzekas, another man who bore watching, and who was giving Gideon a cold eye at that very moment. Still, his report to the ship's captain was obviously and necessarily limited to the real and verifiable.

"Nothing substantive at this point, sir."

Pappas's expression briefly darkened. "I want no surprises, Officer Dayan. When you have something that rises even marginally above conjecture, inform me. You're not alone in your concern about Miss Bennett."

"I will, sir."

"Until tomorrow, then," the captain said, as sure in his dismissals as Gideon was with his own staff.

Gideon nodded, then turned to leave, but the captain's voice turned him back.

"Even marginally, Officer Dayan," Captain Pappas repeated. "Please."

CHAPTER THREE

That afternoon, on an island somewhere off the coast of Italy

ARIANA BENNETT might not have been exactly clear on her current location, but there were a few things that she knew for certain. First, once she was free of her captors, she would never, ever fail to appreciate the luxury of a lavender-scented bubble bath. Actually, at this point, she'd appreciate the luxury of using the facilities without someone listening on the other side of the door.

More importantly, she had come to realize that she was not a peaceable woman. If it took murder to free her from this mess, murder she would commit. And really, murdering a member of the Camorra—assuming that's what her captor was—hardly seemed a crime at all. Mafia was mafia, whether from Sicily, or in this case, Naples. And if he was a smuggler, well, that might make him a lesser star in the constellation of criminals, but he was clearly a kidnapper, too. Bottom line: if it came down to either her or her captor losing their life, Ariana voted for keeping herself alive.

"Are you finished?" Dante, her captor, called through the door.

"That's hardly a question one asks a lady," she called in response, and then thought maybe she heard laughter.

Ariana smiled, but then mentally chided herself for doing so. She was a librarian, and well-read on many topics, including the Stockholm syndrome. She was far too savvy to fall for her captor, even if he did have a few redeeming qualities. In fact, she felt a grudging debt to the man. When his partner, Nico, had held a knife at her throat, ready to kill her, Dante had intervened and given her an injection instead—one she'd thought to be lethal. And now they were in hiding. But why?

She turned on the water tap as a little camouflage for her true activity in the bathroom, and squinted at her iPod screen, trying to make sense of yet another page of her father's notes. She'd transferred them from a disk onto her trusty musical companion, hoping to find a name, a contact, that would help her clear her late father's reputation. It was that belief in Derek Bennett's innocence that had led her to a dig site at Paestum—and her abduction. She didn't want to think what would happen if Dante got hold of her notes.

Of course, even if he did give her iPod more than a basic once-over, it seemed unlikely that he could read Attic Greek, in which her scholar father had written his private notes. Still, she couldn't be too careful. Despite the small kindnesses her captor was showing her, she knew her life was still at risk.

The bathroom's rustic door rattled in its frame as Dante knocked on it. "Three more minutes, Ariana."

"Okay," she called, frowning at the lines of text in front of her. How could twenty-four simple letters confuse her in such a way? Thetas and kappas and omicrons swam in front of her like a college sorority rush list. Her dad had to be scowling from his perch in heaven—or maybe purgatory, at this point—while he watched her trying to recall how to decline an Attic Greek noun. Wasn't it enough to conjugate the verbs?

How could her father have managed to get his name linked to a series of antiquities thefts in the first place? He was a museum curator, not a thief. But he was gone, and she couldn't bear the double loss of both the man and his formerly fine reputation. She would clear his name as her final gift to him. He'd given her so much— encouragement, love and, she wondered now, a genetic tendency to take risks…?

The door shook again. "It is time to come out and find yourself a new game. No more hiding or I will break the lock."

While she didn't kid herself that she knew Dante well, she knew him enough to be sure that he was a man of his word, even if she didn't like those particular words. Ariana turned off the water tap, switched her iPod selection from text to a little Puccini from her eclectic playlist, stuck in her earbuds, then exited the bathroom.

"You push me too far sometimes, you know?" Dante said.

"I can't hear you," she lied over the aria blasting into her head.

He reached out with both hands and tugged loose her earbuds.

"Then watch these lips carefully," he said. "It is not wise to try my patience, Ariana. I want to help you."

She went to brush past him, but he wouldn't let her escape his grip. She hid her fear behind some false bravado. "I can do without your kind of help. You *helped* me into this prison of a house, and I have no idea what you're planning to do with me."

He frowned, his dark brows drawing together, his eyes serious. "In that, you're not alone."

Ariana hesitated, trying to make sense of his frustration. He was the one who'd brought her here, the one who controlled what happened next. Why should he feel as frustrated as she?

"What do you mean? You're the boss. How can *you* be a victim in this?"

Ariana watched as his expression became neutral.

"I mean nothing at all. Listen to your music, Ariana, and give me some peace."

"If you want peace, then let me go," she said, even though she knew the odds of getting that lavender-scented bubble bath were greater.

"In time," he replied. "In time, and in my own way."

Ariana refused to consider exactly what "his way" might be. She cranked up her Puccini, but not even a full-blast aria could hide the pounding of her heart.

This was no bad movie; it was her life, and she was all too well aware of how short that life might be.

LIN KNEW WITH CERTAINTY that Gideon Dayan would arrive at exactly eight-thirty. Since Helga the dragon had left her lair for the day, he had come straight back to her room.

As she did with all who requested her services, she left the room for a few moments to give him the chance to disrobe to the degree that he felt comfortable and to get settled on the massage table. While she stood in the hallway, she worked on her own degree of comfort. She couldn't blame her discomfort on Gideon, either. He'd been slightly distant and yet polite when he'd arrived. He was a client, no different than any other man who had stretched across her table.

"Except for the obvious," she murmured to herself, for she seemed to be having some distance problems herself.

"I'm ready," his deep voice called from the small massage room.

And so I must be, too.

Lin opened the door, then quietly closed it behind her. Her pulse jumped as she looked at him. Despite his scars, he had an undeniably beautiful body. He lay there on his stomach, with his lean, muscled arms bracketing his head, and a sheet draped low over his hips. In the soft light, his skin held a dusky tone—not the pale gold of her own, but more of an olive shade. She already knew how it felt to touch him, and she had to admit that on one level it was a blessing to be able to do so again, even if she should not allow herself the pleasure of that touch.

Ah, pleasure. How very long it had been absent from her life. And how very wrong to seek it in this room.

"Would you like any music?" she asked, thinking that a distraction from what she was about to do would serve her well.

"No more than I did when you asked me the same question five minutes ago."

She could feel color rising on her face and was thankful that he wasn't looking her way. "Yes... Of course."

She turned to her small warming stand and selected an oil that carried just a slight hint of sandalwood, one that Gideon had expressed a preference for the first time she'd given him a massage. After she'd poured a small amount in her right palm, she turned back to him.

"Has your leg been bothering you?" she asked. He had come to her that first time seeking relief from the ache in his upper thigh.

"Not so much my leg as my lower back," Gideon replied, his voice slightly muffled. "I think I've been pushing myself too hard."

Lin smiled. She certainly knew about that. "I think a deep tissue massage would be best, then."

He pushed himself up on his forearms and looked back at her, smiling. "A deep tissue massage from you? I'd think that sturdy Helga would be more the sort."

Lin laughed. "We keep Helga at the desk where she can do no harm. Trust me, I'm strong enough for this task."

His brows arched. "Task?"

She placed the flat of her left hand between his shoulder blades and gently urged him back down. "It was a poorly chosen word."

"Excusable, since it's a safe guess that English isn't your first language."

"Very safe. And you?"

"I grew up bilingual—Hebrew and English. My mother is American by birth, and my father, Israeli. They met when my mother came to Israel one summer during university to volunteer in a kibbutz."

Lin rubbed her hands together, spreading the oil between both, and then placed them on the warm skin of Gideon's upper back. It seemed to her that a current of something—awareness? caution?—passed from him to her when she first touched him.

"A kibbutz?" she asked, trying ever so hard, but failing, to ignore the pleasure rippling up her arms and to her heart. She placed her thumbs on either side of his spine and began a slow and deep downward path to first ease the surface tension from Gideon's back.

"Kibbutzim are communal farming and light industrial communities. It's popular among Jewish students to volunteer at one while traveling in Israel."

She nodded. "Ah." This was a very different farming scenario than what her parents had experienced. They had been coerced into a term of farm labor.

"In any case, my mother ended up making Israel her home, and my two brothers and I have never lived anywhere else."

"Two brothers, eh? Are they as stubborn as you?"

He chuckled. "I am not stubborn, Miss Wang. I simply know what I want."

"That would be another way to regard the issue, I suppose."

"Fair enough. So, do you have any brothers or sisters?"

"No, there's just me. We were a city family, and my parents were strict followers of the law. One child permitted, and they received a girl...not that they have ever once said they would have preferred a boy," Lin quickly added in her parents' defense.

They had been good parents, encouraging her to become the best teacher she could, and quietly disappointed when she ended up taking another path in life. Once she'd gone to Beijing, her life had become her own. They had never met Wei Chan and knew nothing about little Wei. It was safer for them that way.

"I'm sure you were just what they wanted," Gideon said. "How could you not be?"

Lin laughed. "In countless ways. I tried to be the good child, to be respectful at all times, but I wanted a life of my own. I disappointed them."

"No more than any other teenager trying to strike free."

She shook her head. "In some places it's safer to strike free than others."

He was silent for a moment, then said, "I understand."

Lin appreciated the words, for she could sense that they were sincere. She refocused her attention on bringing him at least a physical sort of ease. Since she had no client coming later, she paid no heed to the time and let her hands guide her to the areas where his

muscles sat taut under his skin. And what muscles he
had. His was not the build of a vain man, but one of
someone who appreciated the gift that God had given
him, and tended well to his body. The only marks he
bore appeared to have been inflicted by others, and Lin
knew a moment's anger, again thinking about what one
human could do to another.

She carefully closed away the thought, as she did so
many other dark ones. She imagined that the corridors
of her mind were lined with shiny black lacquered
boxes, each holding thoughts and memories she did not
wish to approach. It had been enough to get past the
memory of Wei Chan's horrible pain prior to his death
without beginning to connect to this man's. She was
best letting it—and him—stay separate from her.

"You can ask, you know," Gideon said in a low voice.

She hadn't realized that she'd paused in her
kneading. Her fingertips rested over a rope of scar tissue
that wrapped to the front of his right knee.

"It is not my place to ask," she replied, pushing back
the curiosity that could spring the latch to one of those
dangerous black boxes. She moved her hands upward
and pressed more strongly into the back of his right thigh.

"Then we'll wait with the answers until it is your
place," he murmured.

Her hands again stilled of their own volition.
"Pardon me?"

But he said nothing at all in return.

Lin drew a breath and busied her hands once again.
Her place? Surely she had imagined that comment, and

if not, how could he imagine that she would ever be privy to his life? And how could she for a moment wish to be?

FIVE HOURS HAD PASSED since Gideon had last been in Lin's presence. Five hours in which he'd chatted with passengers, fielded the usual flirtatious advances from certain women among the staff and thought of nothing but the honey-smooth sound of Lin's voice and the dance of her hands across his skin. Even now, she lingered.

In bed since midnight, Gideon rolled from his back to his side, trying to find a comfortable position in which to rest. He could do without sleep. In fact, he often preferred to, as dreams were not always his friends. But he needed rest in order to be sharp for the coming day.

The white cotton sheets felt rough against his bare skin after Lin's ministrations, and the room was growing too damn crowded for him. He had become accustomed to Rachel's presence in his thoughts. Adding Lin to the mix was leaving him little space to clear his mind. And since Rachel Shalev was a woman of lasting and formidable will, he didn't feel in the least insane for thinking that Lin's presence was annoying Rachel to no end.

Shalev was Hebrew for tranquil, and Rachel could not have had a less fitting family name. She was as tranquil as a typhoon. As subtle as one, too. She had blown into his life when they trained together at Mossad's Intelligence Academy. Rachel was headstrong, brilliant and beautiful, able to retain the smallest detail of whatever she saw or read, and a virtuoso at charming those details out of men and women, alike. Gideon hadn't been immune. Their class work had extended to evening studies together, which had inevitably led to lengthy love-making sessions in his bed…plus a number of more creative places.

He'd been sure that fate had brought them together, and that together they were invincible. For ten years they had loved and fought with equal ardor, right to the end that he'd never seen coming. And though he'd forgiven her for refusing to marry him, and for craving the excitement of her career more than she did the bonds of family, there was one thing for which he could not forgive Rachel. She'd abandoned him empty and alone, with a bitter distaste for heroes and martyrs.

"Fools," he said into the silence of his quarters. As the word hung in the air, he supposed it could apply to him as well as those heroes and martyrs. And when he closed his eyes for the last time that night, Rachel, with her dark eyes and knowing smile, was waiting for him….

Eilat, Israel—sixteen months earlier

GIDEON WAS IN PARADISE, or as close as one could get to it on earth. The Red Sea resort city of Eilat, nestled in the extreme southernmost part of Israel, was sun-drenched, coral-kissed and usually laid-back. But in four days, an international symposium regarding the Arab-Israeli conflict was to be held at one of the city's major hotels. And because Jews and Arabs could not be brought together without a voicing of many opinions,

Israeli students had planned a massive protest march regarding the recent pullout from the disputed territories.

It was rumored among the students that the Palestinian Authority was sending a cadre of very high-ranking representatives to the symposium. Untrue, according to both Israel's and Palestine's governments, but try stopping a rumor among the hot-blooded young in the Internet era. The Israeli government had put out more than their share of official announcements. Rachel and Gideon's wing of the Mossad, which specialized in psychological counterterrorism, had even been pulled in as a last-gasp effort to stop what could be a very inflammatory gathering, but to no avail. The student organizers just kept pointing out that the government had reason to lie. No matter that the government had no such reason at all. The "us versus them" mentality trumped logic every time.

The numbers of people reported to be coming to Eilat to march had been growing exponentially. Gideon, with more than a touch of cynicism, wondered if a great number of them weren't coming more for fun than fervent nationalism. Gideon and Rachel were to be the official face of the Mossad, but their responsibilities were minimal, since the army would be doing the real security work at the march.

He and Rachel had witnessed protests by the dozen around Gaza and the West Bank; security detail was all in a day's work to them. It wasn't so much that they were blasé about their work. They had simply learned that they needed to maintain a real life, too. And since their nation had worked that tenuous cease-fire with the

Palestinians, it seemed that a day at the office had turned into a day at the beach…or in bed.

"Come into the shower, lazy man!" Rachel called.

Facedown on their hotel bed, Gideon groaned. "Lazy? After making love to you for hours?"

This was their first day at the seaside. Despite no official obligations, they hadn't made it out of the room and down to the beach for the snorkeling outing they'd planned.

"Most definitely lazy. That was at least forty-five minutes ago, and we have dinner reservations, so you'd best get moving."

Gideon worked up the energy to turn his head in her direction. She stood in the bathroom doorway, her hands braced on either side of the frame. The love of his life was sleek, naked and so damn beautiful that she could make a man dead with exhaustion hard and ready to have her again.

She smiled as she caught the interest in his eyes. "The shower has possibilities…."

He rolled onto his back, and her smile expanded into a rich laugh as she eyed his growing erection. She pushed away from the door frame and came back to the bed, kneeling above him with her knees to either side of his thighs.

"The shower isn't the only thing with possibilities, is it?" she asked.

"Limited possibilities, my love. I'm not in my twenties anymore," he said, even though his body seemed to think it was.

"Nearly forty, I believe," she teased. "And taking advantage of a younger woman, too."

"I'm thirty-four, as you well know, and the younger woman seems to be taking advantage of me."

She lowered her body over his, leaned down and whispered, "You won't suffer. I promise." Then Rachel Shalev was as good as her word, leaving him gasping and somewhere past spent. He knew to the bottom of his soul that there was no woman on earth whom he could love more.

Once they'd showered and dressed, they were an hour past their dinner reservation, and the hostess at the trendy, glass-walled restaurant built under the Red Sea declined to seat them. Gideon didn't much care. The restaurant had been Rachel's choice; he preferred good, basic food over setting. Since they had ended up at a small café on the fringes of Eilat's North Beach, he had gotten his wish.

"Do you remember being like that?" Rachel asked, with a nod toward an intense young couple two tables over who'd come in just after them and now were in the midst of a spat.

Gideon watched as the younger man reached out and grasped his lover's hands across the table. She was angry, her eyes bright with tears and two flags of red riding high on her cheeks. She moved as though to pull away, but something the man said made her still, then ruefully shake her head and give him a smile that grew stronger when he murmured something else to her.

"It's not so difficult," Gideon replied. "We were like

that this morning, arguing at the airport when we were running late."

Rachel shook her head. "That's not about a missed taxi," she said, with a subtle nod toward the young lovers. "It's about passion…love—"

"Or a credit card bill that came in too high," Gideon finished while taking her hands and mimicking the younger lovers' handhold.

Rachel laughed, then leaned forward, the bold cut of her black dress giving him more than a hint of her full breasts. He met her halfway across the small café table and closed his mouth over hers. Life was beyond good….

GIDEON AWOKE and slowly realized that he was, as ever, alone. His brief sleep had been restless. The sheets were twisted about his legs, and both his pillows had gone over the edge onto the carpeted floor below. His body ached with passion unspent, and his heart ached with loneliness.

She had to let him sleep a full night.

She had to let him go.

Gideon rose from his bed, scooped up the pillows and tossed them back to their proper location, then padded toward the shower. As he stood under the blast of warm water, his body still hard, he heard Rachel's laughter.

She had to let him live again.

CHAPTER FOUR

Midnight...a safe house on the Isle of Capri

WAS THERE SOME SORT of rule shared among the upper echelons of law enforcement that all crisis calls had to take place in the dark of night?

Dante Colangelo snapped shut his cell phone, half wishing he could lob the cursed thing out the window and into the sea. He didn't doubt the accuracy of the information his superiors had just given him. The Camorra had eyes on Capri, and it was quite possible that Ariana and he had been spotted. Logic compelled that *now* was the time to depart. Yet he was reluctant to wake Ariana Bennett and be confronted once again by the accusation and distrust in those blue eyes.

He supposed he would have to shoulder some of the blame for that. After all, he'd kidnapped her, drugged her, lied to her and kept her in the dark, both literally and metaphorically. But this was his job, and he would do it to the very best of his ability.

Of course, he wasn't brimming with trust for his charge, either. Though she had been consistent in her story about why she'd shown up at the Camorra-pirated archaeological dig from which he'd been compelled to save her—that she only wanted to clear her father's name from the stain of being called an antiquities thief—he didn't buy in. She was hiding something, and it was his job to find out what.

Dante headed toward the bedroom door, which she'd kept partially open at his command.

A golden wash of light spilled from the hallway into the dark of the room. He could make out her slender form on the bed.

"Ariana?" he said in a low voice as he neared.

She didn't stir.

"Ariana?"

Still nothing. Dante stepped closer. Was she ill? Worse yet, *dead?*

She'd eaten nothing that he hadn't tasted, and he'd sat outside her bedroom since she'd closeted herself in there, just after their basic Colangelo-cooked dinner of pasta and a green salad. God help his chances for advancement if *la bella strega* died on his watch.

Dante switched on the small bedside light and bent over her. The slow rise and fall of her chest beneath the thin cotton sheet pulled nearly up to her chin gave him some measure of relief. She lived. He was not yet destined to be a babysitter to potential thieves for the rest of his natural life.

Though if all antiquities thieves were as pretty as this one, it wouldn't be too horrible a job. Her lips were slightly parted and her mouth was curved upward in a near smile. He wondered if she dreamed of being kissed, though he'd be more willing to wager that she was dreaming of parting him from his manhood.

"Ariana?"

Though not dead, she slept the sleep of the departed.

Dante settled one hand on her shoulder and gently shook her. She bolted upright and screamed. This was no girlish squeak, but the sort of shriek one might loose with a murderer on one's heels. He yanked his hand back before harm could come to it.

"*Essere tranquillo*…be quiet!" he ordered.

"Hands off!"

He glared down at her, and she glared back. Once again, it was a standoff.

"Get out," she said.

He didn't like the poorly cloaked fear that he saw in her eyes, as if he were some sort of pervert.

"I was trying to wake you," he said. "You must get dressed." Just then he realized that the sheet had fallen, and she wore only a scrap of a bra and not the nightgown that his people had provided for her.

She made a sound close to a hiss as she sank lower in the bed and covered herself once again.

"Seen enough?" she asked, her fear replaced by indignation.

Dante could not help his smile. He shrugged. "I am a man."

"And obviously *not* a gentleman."

His smile grew to a full grin. "And you think that gentlemen don't look? Maybe they are just better at it and do not get caught?"

For a moment, it looked as though she might smile back, and he found himself wishing that she would. Then he reminded himself that watching her was a job, and that would be more easily accomplished if she knew some fear for him.

"Get dressed," he repeated in a flat voice.

"*Now?* But it's the middle of the night!"

"No matter. Dress, or I will dress you." He moved a threatening step closer to the bed.

"Fine! Get out, and I'll dress myself."

"As you wish. And gather what you need from the clothes here. We will not be returning."

"Where are we going?" A telltale quaver marked her voice.

He was a man in all ways, and it was a blow to his gut, hearing her fear. But it was not in his power to comfort her.

"You will just have to wait and see," he said, before turning and walking out the door.

THE NEXT MORNING at 9:00 a.m. Lin sat in Zhang's tiny office space, which was cut out of a corner of the ship's laundry. Wei, content and well-fed, rested in her arms and watched her with bright eyes as she and Zhang conducted the same debate they did at every port.

"How can you not want some time to yourself?" Zhang asked. "You have the required visa, and the spa is closed for a few hours, so go ashore and see the world. Cambro and Awa, especially, have been crying for more time with Wei. They don't work until three o'clock, and could come back to your cabin and play with him."

The two Somali sisters were among Zhang's most trusted helpers with Wei. The girls had been aboard ship since May, working in the laundry to send much-needed money back to their family. They missed their younger siblings and doted on Wei. Lin's son was safe with them, she knew.

The only question that remained was whether she could let go long enough for the feel of solid land beneath her feet. Her few trips ashore had been diffi-cult; she had worried about Wei the entire time. She loved Zhang with all her heart, but her friend was not yet a mother and could not understand the feelings that came with such a position in life.

Zhang heaved an expressive sigh. "This is not a week-long holiday I'm suggesting, but a walk! Take the time for yourself or you're no good to Wei or anyone else."

It was true that Lin had not slept well last night. Wei had been fussy, and in those quiet times when he had slept, she had tried to nap, but her thoughts had contin-ued to drift to Gideon Dayan. She did not truly know him and had great reason to be cautious around him, yet when in his presence, caution flew from her mind. Gideon represented a lack of personal focus that she could ill afford. At least if she left the ship for a few hours, she would not see him.

"This once, I will go, and I'll be back no later than noon."

"Two o'clock," Zhang bargained.

"Noon," Lin firmly replied.

"Fine, then, one o'clock it is," Zhang said with a laugh. She held out her arms. "Now hand me our little warrior, and go get kissed by the sunshine."

Twenty minutes later, Lin waited in line at the crew gangway with the others who were lucky enough to have time to go ashore. She patted her passport case, in which she'd also tucked away some of her precious money. While she'd readied to leave, Wei had again begun to fuss. Much as she hated to admit it, she needed to consider supplementing his feedings with infant formula. She had no idea where in the busy streets of Kusadasi she would find baby bottles and the like, but find them she would.

"So, where do we start?" asked Dima Ivanov, who seemed to have materialized at her side.

"Good morning, Dima," Lin said, neither surprised nor especially pleased that he'd woven through the throng to stake his place next to her. "And start what?"

"We need to start our day of fun, of course. Maybe you would want some wine at a café?"

"I'm only off the ship for a short time. You'd do better to go with some of the others," she replied.

"You need someone to watch over you. I saw you…what's the word?" he asked, pointing at the carpet beneath their feet. "Ah, yes…faint! I saw you faint yesterday."

"I don't faint every day." She racked her mind for an activity that bold and athletic Dima might find boring.

"Really, you need to find a more interesting group. I want only to visit a bookstore and then find a quiet place to read."

"Then I will watch you read."

"Dima, please…"

He looped his arm through hers. "We are friends for the day. And then another day, maybe we will be even better friends, yes?" he asked, accentuating the question with a grin and a waggle of his blond brows.

She had to laugh. "We will be friends today, Dima." As for being more than friends, she was sure she could keep him on the desired platonic path for the two weeks she had left in his company.

Soon they were off *Alexandra's Dream*, into Kusadasi's cruise ship terminal and through customs. They found themselves released to the main part of the building, which was a gleaming new shopping area called Scala Nuova, filled with things Turkish and not-so-Turkish. Lin wanted free of the press and into the streets, which simply had to be less busy, but Dima seemed like a child dropped in the middle of fantasyland.

He took her hand and began to drag her to the left. "Ah, a Burger King! My cousin in Ohio tells me of the Whopper." He stopped, then began to draw her back the other way. "But here I see a bookstore! See, at all times I think of you, Lin."

She wished that he would think considerably less of her, and let go of her hand, as well.

He hauled her toward the store. "I will buy you a book!"

At least she had created a trap of her own liking. While she would rather be out looking for formula, she could not turn down the chance to touch books. She was the child of academics, through and through. While she loved using the Internet aboard ship, nothing would replace the inky scent of a new book or the feel of its pages under her fingertips.

"I will buy my own book, but come browse with me," she offered Dima.

He stopped at the magazine section just inside the door, his eyes apparently drawn to a sporting periodical. Lin ventured on. The small space had tried to cater to all customers, leaving only a handful of books in any one language. While she wandered, Dima still lingered near the doorway, as though the interior of the shop was a humid jungle from which a beast might spring and devour him.

Since there were exactly three books in Chinese, Lin headed to the back of the store, where she found a somewhat larger English section...and Gideon Dayan. His back was to her as he thumbed through whatever tome he'd selected. She considered backing away, but if he turned and caught her taking flight, she would lose what little edge she possessed when dealing with this man.

"Hello, Gideon," she said as she approached.

It seemed to her that he hesitated before turning. "Good morning, Lin."

And when their eyes met, her words flew away. "I...ah, I'm here to buy a book."

He smiled. "That's what most people do in a bookstore."

She'd seen him nearly nude, and she'd seen him in his uniform, but never had she seen him in civilian clothing. In his khaki pants and Mediterranean blue short-sleeved shirt, he seemed almost a stranger to her, and one she found incredibly attractive.

"Yes…well…" *Really, could she do no better than this?*

She grabbed a book from the shelf and began paging through it. The words swam in front of her eyes. It could have been a biography of Winston Churchill or an auto repair guide.

"Will you be taking in the sights?" Gideon asked.

"Shopping…I must shop," she managed to reply.

He laughed. "Must?"

Lin began to relax. "Another poorly chosen word. I *wish* to shop. And you?"

"I wish to do anything *but* shop."

She waved a hand at their surroundings. "Yet here you are."

"Buying books is different than shopping, though, isn't it?"

More and more, she liked his man. "Yes, books are different."

She'd been about to ask him what he'd chosen when Dima appeared. He placed his hand on Lin's shoulder in a gesture that she knew was meant to be proprietary. Had she more room to maneuver, she would have slipped from his grasp. The only place to move, though,

was closer to Gideon, and that didn't seem particularly
wise, either.

"Are you ready?" Dima asked.

Gideon's expression as he took in Dima's hand on
her shoulder was impassive, yet it still somehow made
her feel flat and empty inside. She looked at the book
in her hands. It happened to be a novel by a young
writer she'd been hoping to read, so she closed it and
told Dima that she was indeed ready to leave.

"Enjoy your day," she told Gideon, and he wished her
the same in return. Already, she felt her morning was out
of kilter. Though she didn't want to be romantically
involved with Gideon, she also didn't want him to think
that she was the sort to fall for Dima's surface charms.
But for one morning, she would let those charms enter-
tain her.

Soon they were on the sidewalk, which was marble-
topped, an indulgence that shocked Lin's eyes. She was
far more accustomed to the utilitarian walks of Beijing,
and even of Hong Kong. Here, under a bright morning
sun, jewelers and rug merchants vied for their attention
while luring them with offers of cool mint tea. Dima
laughingly told them to find the rich tourists, not poor
workers. Lin stopped at one shop and bought a jar of
sweet and fragrant orange blossom honey from a
vendor, a luxury to be sure, but not on a par with those
marble walks.

They headed north. After a time the marble gave
way to more pedestrian concrete and narrower streets.
Here, the residents outnumbered the tourists, and Lin

had the sense that she was seeing Kusadasi as it really was. They wandered through a maze of shops selling wares more suited to real life. She began to wonder if she had a chance of actually finding bottles and formula, after all. Lin suggested to Dima that he sit at an outdoor café at the last main intersection they'd passed. He agreed, saying he wanted to try a local beer.

In the third tiny market she entered, Lin found her treasure—powdered formula, bottled water and one baby bottle. She bought the wares and headed back to the café and Dima.

"Show me what you bought," he said once she'd settled in at the small, round table he'd staked as his own.

"It's nothing of interest to a man," she said. "Woman supplies."

Just as Wei Chan had always done when she'd used that phrase, Dima turned the topic elsewhere. "The café owner tells me there's a beautiful park as we go back toward the main shopping area. Let me take you there."

Lin liked the idea of a green space…someplace where she could actually sit and read for a bit before heading back to the ship. Her breasts were beginning to feel overfull, though, and even without looking at her watch, she knew her time ashore was coming to a close.

"That would be lovely. Shall we?"

She began to rise, but Dima held out his hand.

"First, I have one more beer coming."

Lin tallied the three empty bottles already on the table. "The sun has made you thirsty?" she teased.

"I'm Russian. Three beers is nothing. Can I get you one?"

"No, thank you."

"I will hurry, then," Dima said as the waiter set the fourth beer in front of him.

"Take your time." Lin pulled the novel she'd bought from her small bundle of purchases. "I can read for a while."

Dima finished his fourth beer at the same speedy pace Lin suspected he'd finished the other three. And despite his faith in his Russian heritage, he looked a little loose-limbed as he lolled in his chair.

"Would you like some food?" Lin asked, taking a quick look at the English menu the waiter must have left earlier. "I have heard that Turkish cheese rolls are quite good." *And they just might absorb some of that beer.*

"No food—Russian, remember?" Dima replied, thumping his broad chest with the tips of his right fingers.

Lin quelled a sigh and gathered her purchases as Dima paid his tab. She waited as he confirmed park directions, which ended up a garbled mixture of Russian, Turkish and fractured English.

Dima and Lin set off. After only a few false turns, and a few quick moves by Lin to extract her hand from Dima's larger one, they found the park on the edge of the tourist district. It was not a showy place, but had a modest central fountain and several benches at the edge of the square.

Lin's heart jumped when she recognized Gideon

Dayan as the occupant of one of those benches. Head down, he read the book he must have purchased earlier. Some other small packages and a bottle of water sat to his side. If only she had chosen another path this morning, one that would have landed her in this park without Dima.

Dima dug into his pocket and tossed a coin into the water.

"Do you have a wish?" he asked Lin.

"No," she replied, for her wishes would hurt his feelings, and she didn't want to do that.

"I do," he said, trying to draw her closer.

Lin held tight to the packages she carried and anchored her feet more firmly to the ground.

"What's your wish?" she asked with false joviality. Perhaps she could humor him into not intruding on her peace.

He smiled. "A kiss."

She shook her head. "No. It is not respectful." *To me or to the people of this place...*

"Just one kiss," he wheedled. "You're so pretty."

"Thank you, but no, Dima."

Her objections carried no more weight with him than she apparently did. Dima forcibly pulled her closer.

"Be nice, Lin."

She gasped as two of her shopping bags tumbled to the pavement. She turned her head away. "Dima, stop! I don't want to kiss you!"

He pressed his hand against the side of her face and turned her head back.

Lin closed her eyes and tried to block both the sight of him and the sour scent of each of those four beers he'd drunk. The feel of his mouth over hers was a travesty that she fought to end. It might be just a kiss, but to Lin it felt as though she were betraying the love she had shared with Wei Chan. She was a strong woman; she knew she was. But in this moment, her strength fled.

GIDEON HAD SEEN ENOUGH. Lin was no willing participant in Ivanov's embrace, and Gideon had to admit that made him a damn happy man.

He dropped his book on the bench, rose and closed in on the Russian.

"Move away, Mr. Ivanov," he commanded.

The younger man ended the kiss, but he still had one hand wrapped around Lin's upper arm in what had to be a punishing grip.

"Now step clear of Miss Wang."

Ivanov grudgingly complied.

Gideon gave Lin a quick glance to see if any other harm had been done. She appeared shaken, her dark eyes wide and her oval face pale, but otherwise, fine.

"Are you hurt, Miss Wang?" he asked as a formality.

She shook her head, then gasped and bent down to pick up some packages scattered at her feet. Gideon turned his attention back to Ivanov.

"Your behavior is in violation of your employment rules."

"It was a kiss between lovers," the younger man

said. "And we are lovers not even aboard your ship. No rules broken."

Even though he'd seen that the Russian's advances had been unwelcome, Gideon glanced toward Lin. "Lovers?"

"No," she quietly replied.

"Miss Wang tells me otherwise. You are to leave her alone."

The Russian moved closer, nearly into Gideon's face. "You can't tell me what to do!"

Gideon knew that stale scent. It seemed early to be drinking, but staff sometimes ran a little wild despite the cruise line's orders to be sensitive to cultural issues while ashore.

"Did you drink your breakfast, Mr. Ivanov?"

"Bastard!" the man cried, then launched himself at Gideon, who grabbed his arm and twisted it behind the man's back, locking him in a firm grip, with his other arm about the Russian's neck.

"I will let you go, but you should think carefully before you swing again," he advised the Russian, who struggled to free himself.

"You think I cannot beat you, old man?"

Gideon grinned. He might be a decade older than Ivanov and still limited by his injuries, but he had trained in various forms of martial arts and self-defense long and hard while with Mossad.

Gideon tightened his grip, and the younger man gasped.

"Just being sure I have your full attention," Gideon said.

Ivanov nodded.

"Then I will let you go."

The Russian again nodded his assent, so Gideon released him. He rubbed at his throat and gave Gideon a sullen glare.

"And now, Mr. Ivanov, you will return to the ship without another stop along the way. I will not be far behind you to make sure this happens."

Gideon knew enough Russian to understand that Ivanov's response was a foul curse.

"Do you value your job?"

"Please, don't make him lose his job!" Lin cried. "I couldn't bear it."

Gideon saw that she meant it, too. She looked pale and fragile and so incredibly beautiful that he wanted to make her world right for her. She shouldn't have to endure another moment of this strain. He escorted Ivanov several yards away before finishing their one-sided conversation.

"For the rest of this cruise, I don't want to find you within sight of Miss Wang. If you see her heading to the spa while you're going to the Fitness Center, turn away. If she is eating, stay out of the dining room. And if I or my staff see you violate these rules, Mr. Ivanov, you will be leaving ship at the next port. Is that clear?"

The Russian gave his assent, accompanied by another hostile glare.

"You are approximately a ten-minute walk from the ship. Because I am a patient man, I will call ahead and tell my staff to expect to see you in fifteen minutes. If they do not, I will see that you are fired. Still clear?"

"Yes."

"Now, go."

As the Russian stalked off, Gideon pulled his two-way from his pocket and did exactly as he'd told Ivanov he would. Then he returned to Lin, who had gathered all her parcels and now sat on the park bench by his belongings. She was clearly trying not to cry, but tears had begun to spill over her dark lower lashes.

He wished for a tissue to give her, and then recalled the small, gold-and-red-embroidered handkerchief he'd picked up as a souvenir for one or the other of his sisters-in-law. He pulled it from its bag and pressed it in Lin's hand.

"Take this."

"I couldn't."

"Please, keep it. It's all I have to offer." He would have offered his arms to hold her, but he knew that to her, dignity was everything.

She turned the cloth over in her hands. "Thank you. It's very pretty."

His heart turned a little, too, as she used the handkerchief to wipe any evidence of Ivanov's kiss from her lips. Grace under pressure…grace at all times. In her own way, Lin Wang was as strong as Rachel had been.

"You'll see it's even prettier once you wipe the tears from your eyes," he suggested.

Her laugh was a little watery, as well. She stood and walked a few paces away, then turned back to him.

"I'm sorry for being so emotional. Dima was the first after Wei Chan, and if I was ever to be kissed again…" She slipped into silence.

"Wei Chan, he was a lover you left in China?" Gideon asked, trying to sort through what she meant.

"No. My late husband."

Husband? He was certain she'd checked the "Single" box under "Marital Status" in her emergency contact and personal information file, not "Widowed." Not a huge matter, but one that stood out to a man trained to sift through detail.

"I'm sorry for your loss," he replied, for he knew about that to the bottom of his arid heart, even if he'd never persuaded Rachel to formalize their union.

Lin nodded her thank-you.

"He died before—" she began to say, but then stopped. Discomfort rippled across her expressive features. Her eyes grew wide and she began to fuss with the handkerchief, smoothing its red, embroidered edge.

"Before?" Gideon repeated.

"He died before I left China."

"Ah, I see," he said, though he didn't really believe that was what she'd first intended to say. Still, he had no reason to interrogate her, and was surprised and honored that she had offered up this much.

He stood and closed the distance between them.

"A kiss is a very personal thing," she said. "Dima had no right to steal it from me."

"No, he didn't."

She twisted the cloth between her hands. "But he has, and now I can't steal it back."

Gideon thought a moment. "I disagree. You give Dima Ivanov too much power. You can steal back that kiss by wiping it from your mind as you did from your mouth."

"And how do I wipe it from my mind? Your hand-kerchief will be no help there."

"One day, you will find a man you want to kiss, and you will put that memory in the place of Ivanov."

Gideon was relieved to see the corners of her mouth turn upward.

"You are right," she said. "Dima cannot take what I did not freely give. This, though…"

She came closer and settled her hands on his upper arms. "This I give to thank you for your kindness."

She raised herself on tiptoe and brushed her lips against his cheek. It was a delicate whisper of a kiss, just enough to tempt him to draw her into his arms and fully taste her mouth. But he was not a thief like Ivanov. He would not take more than she wished to offer.

But he could hope for more. Much more.

CHAPTER FIVE

At sea that same morning, somewhere in the Mediter-
ranean

ARIANA BENNETT counted her blessings, an act that
took sadly little time to accomplish.

First and foremost, she was thankful that Dante had
removed her blindfold and untied her hands, both steps
he'd had to take last night to get her out of her former
jail and onto this new, floating prison. At least with the
blindfold off, she could fix her vision on an object and
lose the beginnings of the seasickness that plagued her
as the boat—okay, yacht, as this was hardly a fishing
vessel, with its carpet and fine wood finishes—rolled
and heaved.

Second, she was still alive. There had been a few
minutes last night when she'd begun to doubt her intuition that this man didn't really want to kill her. In fact,
after one good shake from him, she'd been scared
enough that she'd fallen silent and become cooperative.
But today was a new day, and the anger that sustained
her was simmering once again.

"So, where are we?" she asked her captor, who was

thumbing through what looked like some sort of girlie magazine. *Figures he'd be one of those,* she thought.

"We are at sea."

"That tells me nothing."

He glanced up from the magazine and gave her a dry look, but no answer.

"Okay, so you're going to be the strong and silent type," she said. "I say strong because I have bruises to prove it."

She twisted one arm toward him and displayed a purplish bruise—the perfect imprint of two fingertips—that had worked its way to the surface since last night.

He looked up again, and as he took in the damage, Ariana thought maybe…just maybe…she saw a glimmer of guilt in his eyes.

"Mi scusi," he replied in a bored tone. "Maybe next time you will fight less."

Okay, so no guilt.

"Well, I'll look at the bright side," she said. "If I escape soon enough, maybe the *polizia* will be able to take a photograph."

"If you are stupid enough to try to escape, remember there are those who want to kill you even more than I do," he reminded.

The problem was, he was right. Ariana nearly laughed as she considered how utterly upside down her world had gone. If a few months ago someone had told her that she'd be mixed up with Italian mobsters…

"Okay, you've put me through my paces in Twenty Questions a couple of times since we…um…met," she said. "Now, I think it's my turn."

He gave a mock yawn, which she decided to take as a sign of assent.

"Question one… Why don't you want to kill me as much as your brothers did?"

He set aside the magazine. "Brothers?"

"Brothers of the blood…in the mafiosi sense, you know? I mean, you have to be a member of the Camorra."

He arched one dark brow at her. "You have a colorful imagination, no?"

"Usually," she conceded. "But I'm seeing mostly red these days. Blood…anger…vengeance…the usual. So are you going to answer my question?"

"I have a higher…how do you say…tolerance for women who talk too much. My brothers, they just kill them. They are widowers many times over."

"Funny."

"You think so?"

"Not really," she said. "Okay, we'll put aside the killing thing for now. Question two… Are you in charge or are you a minion?"

"Minion?" he repeated, rolling the word over his tongue.

Ariana reeled off some synonyms for him. "Down the ladder…bottom-feeder…just following orders, ma'am."

This time he smiled. "No matter what I am, I'm higher up than you, as I am the one giving you orders, no?"

She didn't care if the truth of their relative positions was evident to the universe; she'd never admit to being less than the ruler of all she surveyed…even this tiny salon below deck.

At the very least, she could learn a little about the Camorra's structure, assuming that's who he worked for, so when she got off this blasted boat, she could begin her search to clear her father's name without crossing their path again.

"Back to question two… But we're talking a ladder…right?"

He gave her another of his trademark dry looks. "You are talking. *I* am trying to read."

With that, he picked up his magazine again, but Ariana was not prepared to give up.

"Question three… How many—"

"No question three," he announced.

"But the game is Twenty Questions…not two."

"Abridged version."

Abridged?

Ariana was beginning to believe that Dante's English might be just like the rest of him—not quite as rough as he wanted her to think….

SEAN BRADY loved his job. What guy in his position wouldn't? He had travel, adventure and more women than he knew what to do with. Scratch that last one. He knew what to do with the women.

The job even fed his brain. He'd spent the morning at the Roman ruins of Ephesus, acting as an escort to Father Connelly and his group of passengers. Maybe the priest was more of an entertainer than Sean had pegged him for, and had been just trying to play to his crowd. All the same, Sean had found the priest's presentation a little skewed.

Sure, there were some elaborate brothel ruins at Ephesus. What ancient Roman city couldn't boast a hot brothel or two? And, yes, the brothel's location across from the library ruins was worth a grin. But after that, why had he spent so much time on a side lecture about prostitution through the ages?

And for all the other things Father Connelly had talked about, Sean figured the priest would have dropped at least one reference to St. Paul's letter to the Ephesians, or maybe mentioned the fact that St. John was believed to have spent his last years in the area, and written his gospel while there. That sort of chat fit the collar better than what Sean had heard.

The day had been enough of an oddity that he had to agree with his boss. Something about Father Patrick Connelly didn't ring true...which explained why, instead of taking the front door to the busy tavern he'd just seen the good father enter, Sean was taking the back route.

Barely ten feet wide, the space behind the tavern wasn't an alley in the American sense of the word, but it seemed to be standard for this seedy edge of Kusadasi. As he hid next to a garbage bin just outside the tavern's open back door, Sean distracted himself from the ripe odor of rotting fish by mentally listing Turkish things.

Turkish baths... He'd be ready for one after hunkering down here. He rose slowly and took a peek into the kitchen. It was a "no go" of an entrance for him, with a surly cook over the stove, a cigarette dangling from his lips. Sean slipped by the door, ignoring the shaggy gray cat that had come out to greet him—or maybe guard its territory.

Turkish towels... Were they terry cloth or something? How was he supposed to know? Sean scoped out the rest of the building's backside. Other than knocking out the cook and getting a little more ash in the patrons' food, he could see no way of gaining entry here.

Less than three feet separated the tavern from its neighbor to the north, but Sean would take three good feet over the cook any day.

Turkish prisons... Thanks, but no thanks, on that one. He edged down the narrow passageway, which, with its litter of broken chairs and tables, also seemed to serve as some sort of burial ground for the tavern. About eight feet into the maze, he caught a break. There was a half-opened window in easy reach.

Sean crept below the window. It wasn't to the tavern's main room, or he'd be hearing one helluva lot more noise. He waited a few moments longer. As he lingered, his nose alerted him to what he was about to face.

Turkish bath...room.

Once he was sure the place was empty, Sean tried to work the window open a fraction more, holding his breath as the dry wood rattled in its frame. *Come on, no noise, baby...*

Finally, the window cooperated. He hoisted himself inside, this time holding his breath at the smell. He'd known he wasn't climbing into the Ritz, but no matter how basic the facility, a little soap and water never hurt.

With more speed than grace, he exited the bathroom and paused just outside the door. A short hallway separated the bathroom from the dining area. The dim and smoky place was fairly crowded. There appeared to be a smattering of what looked to be other nations' soldiers on leave, which was good news for him. He'd blend in as well as he could hope to.

Sean took a seat at a table for two along the back wall. It hadn't been cleared since its prior occupants had left, which also suited his purposes. He picked up a section of the newspaper which the last diner must have been reading and used it as more camouflage.

Three tables in front of him sat Father Connelly, downing a beer. The man was by himself, and like Sean, had a newspaper to occupy him. Pretty mundane stuff, all around. Then again, much of surveillance was just that—dull and mundane. Sean hunkered in for the wait, pulling a wad of Turkish lira from his pocket and sticking them on the tabletop, just in case a waiter arrived and he needed to buy some time.

He watched as Connelly chatted up the little waitress who had just brought him a plate of *mezes*. Friendly guy. *Maybe a little too friendly,* he mentally added as he caught the waitress's rather shocked expression when she turned away.

Sean went back to his newspaper while Father Connelly wolfed down his appetizers. He was about to officially declare this leg of his surveillance a bust when someone familiar came through the tavern's front door.

Damned if it wasn't First Officer Tzekas...

Sean tuned up his hearing a notch. Life aboard ship, with its smaller confines and number of people, had sharpened his skills at sorting out background noise. This place was also short on English-speakers, so anything the priest had already said had stood out.

Giorgio Tzekas pulled out a chair and sat. "Does the boss know where you were today?"

The priest took a long draw of his beer before answering. "We both know the boss knows everything."

Sean frowned. He had to assume that they were talking about Captain Nick Pappas, but no one aboard ship referred to him as "the boss." Those fired employees who Sean occasionally had to escort off *Alexandra's Dream* had saltier names for him, and the rest stuck with Captain.

"I've been leaving you messages. Why don't you return them?" Tzekas asked.

Sean had a sudden vision of Tzekas as a jilted girlfriend and had to bite back a laugh.

"I told you to meet me here," Father Connelly replied. "That's returning a message, isn't it?"

"Too little and almost too late. Megaera has been looking for you. Did you do any shopping?" the first officer asked.

Meg-who? Weirder and weirder, Sean thought.

"I led a tour and then I came here," Father Connelly said, then popped a small piece of sausage into his mouth.

Whatever Tzekas said in reply was lost in the rattle and clatter of the waiter clearing an adjacent table. Sean leaned a bit in the direction of his shipmates, trying to pick up on the conversation once again.

"...to piss the boss off," Father Connelly was now saying.

The man didn't exactly strike Sean as the diligent sort. Neither was he a permanent employee of the line. But Sean would just absorb their conversation now, and try to apply meaning to it later.

Fate had another plan in mind, though. The waiter who had been clearing the nearby table slipped, sending his tray crashing into Sean as the man tumbled to the floor. The sounds of shattering glass and breaking crockery silenced the tavern. Sean froze, hoping against hope that Connelly and Tzekas hadn't turned his way. They had, of course. His eyes met Tzekas's, and he knew he'd been made.

Sean stood, brushing off the remnants of another diner's meal with the used napkin the waiter offered him. He accepted the waiter's apology—"sorry" in a litany of languages—and assured him that he was fine. There was nothing to do but leave.

As he passed the men at their table, Father Connelly stopped him.

"I didn't see you in here, Sean," he said. "Sorry about the bit with the waiter."

"It's no big deal. Not too much damage. Great tour today, by the way," he added.

"Won't you have a seat?" the priest offered, while

Tzekas, who was already under Security's eye for some violations of ship rules, scowled at the tabletop.

"No, really," Sean said. "I think I've already tried— or worn—everything on the menu. It's time to get back to the ship."

"Well, have a good evening, then."

Sean nodded his goodbyes to the men and headed out through a more traditional and less pungent entrance to the tavern than the one he'd tried earlier. And all the way back to *Alexandra's Dream* he played that fragment of conversation through his head.

The boss...

If not Captain Pappas, then who?

MEGAERA WAS NOT HAPPY, and when the boss was not happy, no one beneath her stood a whisper of a chance for happiness, either. One name—one very unacceptable name—had popped up on her computer screen as she perused the latest information regarding activities aboard *Alexandra's Dream* that her contacts had been able to supply.

Ariana Bennett had still not returned to the cruise ship.

She leaned back in her chair, lit a cigarette and drew in deep. Some days it seemed that her plans were unraveling, fool by fool. Ariana Bennett, fool that she was, was also Derek Bennett's daughter.

Megaera turned back to her computer and began to type an e-mail to one of her contacts, this one a Greek with Interpol, hopefully less a fool than the others she'd been forced to use to see her scheme to fruition.

Please investigate whereabouts of Ariana Bennett,
daughter of Derek Bennett, and last employed as librarian on *Alexandra's Dream*, Liberty Line. Imme-
diate response is appreciated.

CHAPTER SIX

IF GIDEON WERE TO GRADE his day ashore for its effectiveness in removing Lin Wang from his thoughts, he'd have to mark it a total flameout of a failure. She was in his mind, and now on his skin. There was no denying that he wanted her in his bed. He wanted *inside* her; he could devour her whole. Except that he was a civilized man, a trait that he was proud of in most instances, but that chafed a bit just now.

"Focus," he reminded himself.

As he did several times a day, Gideon paged through the incident reports logged into the ship's security system. Lost passport…poolside slip and fall on the Artemis deck…spousal lockout, Hermes deck…stray baby…

Gideon paused, then looked again. "Stray baby?"

In his months aboard ship, this was the first time he'd seen that particular heading on an incident report. If it were a lost baby, he'd have heard well before now, but a *stray* baby?

He moved his mouse and clicked on the detail button. Apparently, someone on the housekeeping staff had reported hearing a baby in a cabin below deck, an area where only crew and staff would be housed. Clearly, crew and staff did not come aboard toting babies.

"None found" was the extent of the detail the investigating officer had provided.

Curiosity—and frustration—piqued, Gideon picked up the phone, called the investigating officer and asked him to come to his office. In only a few minutes, Hank LaFave, another American on the security team, arrived.

"So, a baby below deck?" Gideon asked.

"That's what was reported, sir," replied LaFave, a laconic Texan who always favored a few words over many, as the "detail" from his earlier report indicated.

"Officer LaFave, I do not expect a novel as part of an incident report. Neither do I expect to still have questions when I'm through reading."

The officer straightened his posture to one nearly military. "Yes, sir."

"Please tell me the substance of the report and what you found."

"One of the household staff reported hearing a crying infant at approximately eleven hundred hours. I went to investigate, but heard nothing. I checked cabins in the area of the reported noise, but they were either vacant, or those that were occupied had no babies, sir."

"And that, Officer LaFave, is what your report should have said. Now you may go."

The young man looked relieved when he realized that this was to be the full extent of his dressing-down. "Thank you, sir."

After LaFave had left, Gideon considered the logical

possibilities for someone having heard a baby. They'd been at port until six in the evening, which meant that someone on the crew might have had a visitor. Except no friends or family should have been aboard without prior clearance, and none had been granted.

Another possibility was that a travel agent had come aboard as part of a sales tour...a frequent occurrence on *Alexandra's Dream*. That, too, had to be ruled out, though. The areas below deck were not part of a standard tour. They would do nothing to convince a travel agent to promote the ship as the ideal vessel for a cruise. Casino and pools, yes. Crew quarters, no.

Those ideas exhausted, Gideon checked the passenger list. There were exactly three babies among the nearly one thousand passengers aboard ship. A small number, but in keeping with their current ports. Most parents wouldn't be interested in carrying a child uphill and down as they hiked the ruins ringing this part of the Mediterranean. He cross-checked the list against those who had disembarked for tours or time ashore today. All three babies had not been present on the ship.

"Curious," Gideon murmured. But not exactly the stuff that security alerts were made of, either. If one lucky crew member had been able to sneak a relative aboard for a meal and some fun, so be it.

Gideon tried to close his mind to the topic, but one word kept wriggling its way back in. Babies.

He'd had so little contact with babies. Both of his younger brothers were married and had families. Gideon's time with them had been limited to holidays and an annual family dinner that his mother compelled all Dayans within two days' travel time to attend. His nieces and nephews had been fine babies, the few times he'd seen them at that stage. They'd been plump and sassy, and he'd actually enjoyed holding them, right up until it came time to change a diaper.

Rachel, on the other hand, had always found a way to avoid holding babies. She was busy helping Gideon's mother, or she'd claim she was coming down with a cold. He had known that babies weren't in her plans, and he had loved her enough that he'd been willing to wait and see if one day she might change her mind. And if she didn't, he would have kept on loving, anyway...

Eilat, Israel, sixteen months earlier

OVERNIGHT, Eilat had donned a coat of posters and flyers, all touting the student march two days off. Youth hostels had begun to fill, and the town had taken on a decidedly collegiate edge. For the first time ever, Gideon felt old. Damn old. But his vision was as good as ever.

"Across the street—isn't that the couple we saw at the café the night we arrived?" Gideon asked Rachel as they walked down the main strand toward their hotel.

Over the past two days, Gideon and Rachel had met with the mayor, the military spokespersons and the symposium planners, giving them the key phrases to use to keep the crowds calm—"free and open exchange of ideas," "your voice is being heard" and the like. Still, they had found time to go snorkeling, swim and sun on the beach until Rachel was as golden and beautiful as he'd ever seen her. Tomorrow, before the true madness began, they hoped to pack in a short scuba diving tour.

But semivacation or not, Gideon still had his instincts, and he found it unsettling that in a town now overrun by students, they'd see the same couple yet again. He wasn't so sure whether it was equally odd— or just an indicator of their relationship—that the couple was arguing again. They were dressed in the uniforms Gideon had seen at his and Rachel's hotel, as though she was a maid and perhaps he was in maintenance.

Rachel danced in front of Gideon, then halted him with hands on his shoulders and a quick kiss on his mouth. "Relax. I doubt they're following us. We're simply not that interesting, Mr. Dayan."

Gideon slowed as the couple rounded a corner and turned down a side street.

Rachel gave a resigned sigh. "Fine, if you're so curious, let's just see where they're going."

She tugged his hand and told him to hurry or they would miss the gap in traffic and not be able to cross the road in time.

"Admit it. You're curious, too," Gideon teased.

She laughed. "I'm not curious. More trained like a good little automaton. You can take the woman out of the office, but you can't take the office out of the woman."

Office—that was their joking term for what they did. Their "office" might not be among the secretive paramilitary of Mossad's Metsada division, but they were hardly low-level clericals, either. Though they reported to different supervisors, Gideon was above Rachel in the chain of command, which, she said, made it only fair that she be in charge at home. Gideon suspected that she'd have been in charge, in any case.

They crossed the street and then turned down the same street the couple had taken, staying far enough back that only another expert would have detected them as tails. The tourist area eventually gave way to residential. Rachel and Gideon slowed as the couple headed up the walk to a small apartment building.

"See?" Rachel said. "They're residents. Nothing more. Now let me call the dive shop and confirm that we're still scheduled for tomorrow, okay, Office Man?"

Gideon smiled for her, but his sense of discomfort lingered.

He and Rachel continued their stroll by the building the couple had entered. His unease grew when he saw the young woman peeking out at them from behind the drawn drapes of a second floor window.

He said nothing to Rachel, who was on her cell with the dive master. Instinct seldom failed him, and instinct told him that all was not well. It was a damn shame that instinct couldn't also tell him exactly what was wrong.

"INSTINCT," Gideon said aloud, now lifetimes and miles from the resort city of Eilat. There were times when it seemed almost better to go blindly through life, surprised by one event and the next, rather than have instinct there to warn a man. After all, the end results were frequently the same.

After checking the video monitors one last time, Gideon rose and left his office. He knew that tonight he'd walk this ship's halls a very, very long time before he would sleep.

Soon, though, he would let her go, for it wasn't just Rachel holding on to him.

THE NEXT MORNING, Lin glared at her flushed reflection in the mirror above her small sink, then turned around to face her friend Zhang, who sat cross-legged on the cabin's empty bed, playing with Wei.

"*What* was I thinking?" she cried.

Zhang laughed. "That you wanted to kiss Gideon Dayan's cheek, perhaps?"

She held her hands to her heated face. "Even if I did, it was wrong of me! So wrong!"

"Would you please not be so critical of yourself? You are young and alive, and it's only natural that a man should interest you."

"I have no time for this sort of nonsense!"

"Which makes it all the better. Steal your kisses, remember that you are alive, and then move on to Paris and start your life again."

But Lin wanted more than kisses. Much, much more. And she was not at all the sort to give her body without engaging her heart. She was so wary of the connection she felt growing between the two of them that yesterday, before reboarding the ship, she'd even made

Gideon take back the handkerchief he had tried to give her. Her face colored with embarrassment as she recalled her shrill insistence. What he'd do with it now that it was all tearstained and rumpled, she didn't know.

She flung herself onto her own bed. "This is such a mess!"

"A mess? A mess would be wanting to kiss that Ivanov again. Better you kiss Gideon Dayan than Dima Ivanov."

Lin had to laugh. "Much better, indeed."

She went to Zhang, scooped up Wei and smiled into his round face. Lin popped out his pacifier and gave him a gentle kiss on the forehead. She wondered if he would ever look anything like her...if perhaps cheekbones like hers were hidden behind the weight he seemed to carry only in his face. For now, he was his father, down to the cowlick in his hair.

"Have you spoken to Gideon since that kiss?" Zhang asked.

She winced at what had happened even prior to her odd behavior over the handkerchief. "Yes. We had to walk all the way back to the ship together, both of us wanting to talk about that kiss, but not wanting to in the same breath." She paused, almost hating to say the next aloud. "We talked of the weather."

Zhang laughed. "Very romantic of you."

"I'm a mother! I know nothing of romance."

"Then it's a wonder that you became a mother in the first place," Zhang teased.

Lin refused to think anymore of Gideon Dayan!

She picked up the bottle of powdered formula and spring water that she'd been warming under the sink's hot water tap for Wei. Thank heaven for the pictures on the fat can of powdered formula, for she at least had a hope that she'd mixed the bottle in the correct proportions. If this switch to formula worked, she'd have to "borrow" from the stock of bottled water she kept for clients, but feeding her child came before this small blow to her honor.

"It's time to try something new, my little warrior." She sat on the bed and rubbed the nipple against Wei's lower lip. As he was hungry, he rooted for it and took it into his mouth.

Ah! Perhaps this would be easier than she'd anticipated!

Wei then grunted and turned his head away from the nipple, giving her a look that Lin could only interpret as *do you take me for a fool?*

So much for easy.

"Give it a chance," she crooned as she again rubbed the nipple against his lip. "It's good and will fill your tummy."

He turned his head and screwed up his face in what she knew was a precursor to one of his protest squalls. Lin stood and began to softly bounce him.

"Shh, my sweet, my love. No crying."

Zhang, ever practical, walked to Lin's bedside and turned on the small compact disc player that Lin's former roommate had left for her. Soft music filled the room.

"No rock and roll?" Zhang asked. "No music with screamers?"

"None," Lin said, not looking away from Wei. Eye contact seemed to always quiet him.

Zhang shook her head. "You will have some by tonight. This wouldn't block the cries of a mouse."

And Wei was small, but no mouse.

"Let me have him," Zhang said. "He might take the bottle from me, since he knows I have nothing else to offer him." She patted her rather flat chest, and added, "Obviously."

Lin sighed. "It won't hurt to try, will it?"

"No. And our little warrior looks pained enough, already."

Wei did, indeed. He looked downright insulted that his mother should be depriving him so.

Zhang took Wei, then held out a hand for the bottle. Lin watched as she expertly persuaded the nipple into Wei's little mouth. He sucked hungrily once, then gave an openmouthed grimace and let the formula run out.

"Is the taste not to your liking, your highness?" Zhang murmured to the child. "Perhaps you just need to give it another chance?"

He began to whimper, and Lin felt like whimpering, too.

"Is this how a warrior behaves?" Zhang asked the baby. "Is this how the son of the revered Wei Chan wants to start his life?"

She touched the bottle's rubber nipple to his mouth one more time. Wei took it. Lin knew she should be happy, but she also wished he would have done it for her. One milestone given up to another… It was a selfish thought, but in her struggle to get to Paris and pick up Wei Chan's work where he'd left off, she had already given up so many other moments that a mother and child should share. This was not Zhang's fault, though. It was fate. Capricious and unkind fate.

Zhang handed the baby back to Lin, then settled down on the edge of the spare bed. "I have some news I need to share with you."

From her friend's tone, Lin knew this was not good.

"What is it?" she asked.

"A letter caught up with me yesterday. It was from my cousin Tao, in Jiangsu."

Lin's heart beat more quickly. Wei Chan had been born and raised in that village; his parents still lived there.

"It seems there's a rumor floating about the village that Wei Chan fathered a child before he died. Tao knows that Wei and I were close. She's asking me what I know," Zhang said.

Lin nodded as she held tighter to her child. She had known that it was an impossibility to have baby Wei go through life undetected. Still, though, she had hoped that she would be able to create a safe harbor for the two of them by the time Wei Chan's parents discovered the truth.

"Please don't start worrying yourself," Zhang urged.

Lin gave a choked laugh. "I haven't stopped worrying myself since Wei Chan was released from interrogation and so quickly fell ill. This? This is just more of the same."

"Remember, not Tao or anyone else in the family knows you're here on the ship with me. This was just family gossip that Tao thought I might be able to embellish."

"But if it's gossip in Jiangsu, Wei Chan's parents are involved, somehow. The village is too small for anything else to be true," Lin said.

"That is likely," Zhang agreed. "But of little import. You are safe here, Lin. I can think of no place safer."

Lin could. Paris. If she could get to Paris, Wei Chan's compatriots would help shield her child. It had always been her plan to go back to her homeland, but only under her terms, and when she could best effect a change by bringing publicity to Wei Chan's cause. She knew that the publicity could well come at the cost of her freedom or her life, which was why she needed her child better sheltered. To be with Wei Chan's parents would be a prison to baby Wei, and anathema to everything his father stood for.

"Stop looking like the world is about to end," Zhang said. "I will go into an Internet café in Bodrum this morning and see what I can learn from my contacts within the organization."

Though she knew that Wei Chan's group had eyes even in Jiangsu, Lin felt frozen with indecision. "But isn't it dangerous if you contact them? What if—"

"No what-ifs. You know that we have safe sites and safe e-mail addresses set up for just this sort of issue. I won't be endangering you, I promise."

Lin shook her head. "I know…I know…it's just—"

Zhang placed a steadying hand on her shoulder. "Please breathe. You can't keep this up. Life being what it is, I doubt I'll hear anything today, and if you work yourself into a state, you're no good for anyone. Especially that baby in your arms."

Zhang was right, of course. Yet knowing one should be calm and actually achieving that calmness were two different things. Lin could feel Wei tense in her arms, as though her worries flowed through to him. She closed her eyes, drew air to the very bottoms of her lungs and tried to focus on a comforting scene, like being a child at the dinner table with her parents in Harbin. Instead, she kept seeing Gideon…the way slight wrinkles radiated outward from the corners of his eyes when he gave one of his rare smiles, and the way his rougher male face had felt against her lips. Ah, well, she could do worse for an image to center her.

When she opened her eyes, Zhang was looking at her curiously.

"Shall I ask what you saw behind your eyelids, or by your smile, shall I assume that it was Gideon Dayan?" Zhang asked.

Just then their coded series of knocks sounded at the door, saving Lin from more teasing.

"It's either Cambro or Awa," Zhang said as she walked to the door. "They're here to watch your little warrior. I taught them our door code, since I knew I'd be going ashore."

She looked through the spyhole to be certain of her

visitor, and then admitted Cambro, who quietly greeted Lin and Zhang. The tall and lovely young Somali woman then came to Wei and stroked her fingers across his silky black hair as he finished the last of his bottle.

"You take the bottle so nicely," she said to the child, then focused on Lin. "I am glad to have another way to stop him from crying besides the pacifier. It was a very close thing, yesterday."

Maybe she'd finally centered her mind, or maybe she'd just reached that unfortunate state where nothing more could rock her, but Lin's heart didn't even jump at this comment.

"What happened?" she asked.

"Our young man was feeling unhappy and started to cry yesterday morning. I amused him as quickly as I could, but someone out in the hallway heard him. A woman came knocking at a number of the doors in the corridor. When she was gone, I quickly took Wei to your spa room and used the passkey that Zhang left for me, as I knew the room was closed for the morning."

"Very good," Zhang murmured.

Good? Yes. Cambro had done as well as anyone would have in the same situation. But, incident by incident, the fates were delivering Lin a message.

Time was running out.

CHAPTER SEVEN

On a yacht somewhere in the Mediterranean

"Is THERE STILL A SUN?" Ariana asked her captor as they sat in a windowless salon that she'd describe as being located somewhere in the yacht's bowels, except that it really was a pretty attractive space.

"Yes there is a sun, but do not ask to see it for yourself."

Close, but no cigar. What she was really shooting for was solitude. She glanced down at her very best friend—her iPod. Before Dante had shooed her from her cabin for breakfast and an unabridged game of Twenty Questions—with him as the questioner—she'd been making some progress with her father's notes.

"Could I ask, then, that I get maybe twenty minutes to myself? You know, a little alone time?"

Did she imagine the brief flash of hurt that chased across his features?

A knock sounded at the salon door. Dante rose and opened it a crack. Ariana tried to get a peek at whoever was on the other side, but Dante's broad back made that impossible. He and the visitor held a conversation in

Italian, spoken so quickly and in such a low tone that she couldn't pick up anything useful.

Dante closed the door and turned back to her. "You will have your minutes of 'alone time.' And I will be locking this door, so do not think you will be going exploring."

Once he had left, she glanced at the closed door. It was a weird thing, but she might actually miss Dante a little when this was all over.

For now though, she had to make use of her time alone. Ariana toggled her iPod until she was back in her father's file. Just in case Dante might walk in, she also stuck in her earbuds to make it look as though she were really listening to music.

Ariana frowned at the small screen. Sorting through the information her father had left had been hard enough on a computer screen. This miniature wonder made it a real struggle. Still, one thing kept coming clear: the letter combinations of tau kappa and alpha kappa. She was fairly sure they were place-fillers for something…places or contacts her father might have had, perhaps. The more she looked for some pattern, though, the less the letters on the screen made sense. After a few more minutes, Ariana switched off the iPod and set it aside. She'd look at it later. It wasn't as though her dance card was full…

THE LAST TIME Gideon had actively wooed a woman was at university in Tel Aviv, a lifetime ago. Back then, a guy invited the target of his wooing to the disco, maybe bought her a dinner, and hoped for the best.

On the heels of graduation had come his stretch in the military. Because of the dangers inherent in his particular duties, it hadn't seemed fair to do any wooing. After all, a woman liked to know where her lover was, and if perhaps he might come home in the next month or so. So, he had stuck to relationships that had more to do with mutual physical satisfaction than a future together.

And then there had been Rachel—no wooing required, just a bracing of one's knees as she threw herself at him, full force. Gideon shook off the past and focused on the present. Actually, presents...

When he'd awakened this morning, his first thought had been of Lin pressing that crumpled handkerchief back at him. He'd lain abed and considered why she wouldn't keep it. Pride, perhaps? A need to reject the memory of Ivanov's kiss? No matter, Gideon had finally decided. It was *his* selfish need that she have something he'd given her—something she could look at and think only of him.

This morning he had no time to venture ashore to see what Bodrum might have to offer. His office was drowning in a sea of paperless paperwork. And so here he was, standing outside the cluster of boutiques on the Bacchus deck, not in an official capacity, but in the foreign territory of a customer.

Over the years, Gideon had grown to know what Rachel had liked—perfume, simple earrings, gadgets for the kitchen and anything remotely related to sport. He had no idea what Lin Wang might desire. He only knew that he desired her. Gideon looked at the array of items in each of the shops' small front display windows.

Lingerie? Hardly. At least, not yet. After all, a man had to be optimistic.

Clothing? Mundane.

Jewelry? As long as it was nothing so expensive that she would refuse it. Gideon neared the window.

He'd been there just a few seconds when a familiar voice sounded beside him.

"Of all the places I never thought I'd find you, this tops the list," said Sean Brady. "Pulling out the big guns for a lady, eh?"

"Window-shopping," Gideon replied, using a stern tone that he hoped would dampen Brady's curiosity. No such luck, though.

"You don't window-shop. Hell, other than a book or some booze, I've never seen you buy a thing in all the time we've worked together."

"I'm branching out," Gideon said drily.

"Must be a pretty fancy tree, considering all the glitter in that window."

Gideon said nothing, because that was exactly what Brady needed to know.

"So, did you have a chance to look at my report from yesterday?" the younger man asked, in what Gideon considered a very wise change of topic.

"Yes. It's interesting that Father Connelly and Tzekas would meet up off the ship."

"Agreed," the American replied. "It's clear they've got something going on."

Gideon nodded. "Just keep watching them, and let me know if you see anything else out of the ordinary."

"Say, like seeing you staring into a jewelry store window?" the security officer asked with a grin.

"That will be *all,* Brady," Gideon said firmly, fighting back a smile at the American's infectious good nature.

Once Gideon was sure that Brady wasn't lurking in the shadows, he stepped into the store. There had been one piece with more substance than glitter in the front window.

"Good morning, sir," said the shopkeeper—Maura from Ireland, according to her badge.

"Good morning, Maura. I'd like to know about that carved pendant in the window."

"Ah, you must be talking about the white jade piece," said the woman. "Grand, isn't it? Let me get the window key and I'll show it to you."

While she retrieved the pendant, Gideon gave a cursory look around the shop to see if there might be anything else that suited Lin, but he already knew he'd found the ideal item.

Maura set the jade on a black velvet display pad. "This is a reproduction of a piece from the Qing Dynasty, which means it has all of the beauty of the original, but it's not nearly so dear."

"Do you mind?" Gideon asked, reaching out to touch the necklace.

"Not at all," the shopkeeper replied.

He took the delicate disk between two fingers and

marveled at the intricate carving of a dragon ringed by small birds. Strength and delicacy…

As he looked closer, he noted a tiny streak of very light green running through the stone that only enhanced the necklace's beauty. He could see it now against Lin's skin. He turned over the small price tag attached to its fine gold chain and saw that he could even afford it.

"I'll take it," he said, speaking before he could let reason overrule the need to give Lin something from him.

After finishing his purchase, Gideon let the same need drive him to the elevator and to the Helios deck, where he knew he would find Lin working. Gift bag in hand, he greeted Helga at the spa's reception desk.

"Is Miss Wang with a client?" he asked.

The receptionist eyed the bag speculatively. Gideon raised his brows and gave her a flat look, daring her to step out of line.

Helga moved her gaze to her computer screen. "She's free at the moment. Do you wish to schedule an appointment?"

"No, I just wish to have a word with her. Would you please call her and tell her that I'm on my way back?"

"I will, sir." She lifted the phone's handset.

Gideon knew that he should wait to be announced; it was the polite thing to do. But the same need that had pushed him from sleep and then later to the jeweler's was still strong in his blood. Manners could wait until after he'd seen Lin Wang again.

LIN'S TELEPHONE RANG, and she scowled at the shrill invader. Gideon had certainly seen that she was plugged back in in a hurry. She wished she could unplug the horrible thing. This was to be her half hour of peace, since she'd already dashed back to her cabin and worked with Cambro to get more of that hated formula into Wei's tummy.

"Go away," she said a little crankily.

Since Lin hadn't nursed, her breasts were full and hard, and even her teeth ached with the need to feed her son. She'd known that she would have to go through this sooner or later, but later was sounding a far better idea than sooner.

Ignoring the phone, Lin reached into the storage cupboards built into the back wall of the massage room and pulled out a towel. She would express just enough milk so that she wasn't in pain. That seemed a decent compromise…at least one that would get her through a few more hours.

She pulled her polo shirt from her pants and had just reached behind her back to unclip her bra when a knock sounded at the door. She let her frustration escape in a hiss and then called that she'd be right there. Lin tugged her clothing back in place, not bothering to tuck in her shirt. She should have answered that demon phone, after all. Then the person outside—no doubt controlling Helga—would have left her alone.

She smoothed her shirt one last time and then opened the door. Instead of Helga, though, it was Gideon Dayan. More startling, in his right hand he held a gift bag...one that she knew came from the ship's jeweler.

"May I come in?"

"Yes, of course," she said. How she wished she'd pulled herself together a little more before opening the door.

Once Gideon was in the room, she closed the door and offered him a seat in her sole chair, which he declined. Lin needed more space for her mind to work properly. She moved to the opposite side of the massage table.

"Did you sleep well last night?" she asked, grasping for some semblance of casual conversation.

"Not really." He circled around to her side of the table. "I've, ah...brought you something," he said.

She raised a hand as though to halt him. "Really, I couldn't. It wouldn't be proper."

"How?"

"How, what?" she stammered. The room seemed to be growing smaller and warmer by the second.

"How would it not be proper? We're friends, and I want you to have something from me."

"Then I don't suppose you'd like to offer me the handkerchief again?"

He laughed. "No, I'd like to give you this."

Gideon reached into the bag he held and pulled out a long box wrapped in metallic gold and blue paper.

"I can't," Lin said, her voice shaking.

"How do you know until you look?" Gideon asked. "Go on, at least unwrap it."

She supposed it wouldn't hurt too much to do that.

When she took the box from him, their hands brushed. She glanced up at him and their gazes locked. It was, bar none, the most intimate moment Lin had experienced since Wei Chan's death.

He smiled at her. "We might both survive this, yet."

She smiled back, then turned her attention to the box. While she unwrapped it, he carefully folded the gift bag and set it on the massage table. His actions were deliberate, almost as though he was trying not to become too invested in her reaction to his gift.

Paper joined bag on the massage table, and Lin took the top off the gold-covered box that had waited beneath. She gasped, for she never would have expected something so perfectly suited to her.

"It's beautiful, Gideon," she meant to say, but her voice came out a whisper.

The disk of white jade was about the size of the American half-dollar that an elderly client had once given her, and carved with a bold dragon in the middle and swallows floating about the outside. A line of green ran through the jade as though marking it with the earth's blessing.

Lin was quite certain she'd seen a piece like this somewhere before, in a glossy book on Chinese antiquities which Ariana Bennett had given her to read.

"It was like you, both strong and delicate." He looked down at the floor, as though embarrassed by his words. "It's a reproduction of an old work."

Lin set aside some of her nervousness in the face of his equal discomfort. "Thank the heavens for that! If it were the original, you'd be scooping me off the carpet as I fell into another faint. I've seen the original in a book that my friend Ariana once loaned to me," she explained. "I know it would be very valuable…not that this isn't to me!"

How graceless can one woman be in accepting a gift? she silently chided herself.

"You're going to keep it, then?"

She held the box to her chest. "How could I not? It's perfect! You must have known the connection."

"Connection?"

"My name… It means beautiful jade."

He looked startled. "Really?"

She nodded. "Yes. So you knew of the warrior Ng Mui, but not of beautiful jade?"

"Martial arts have been a constant part of my life, and beautiful jade not so very much…until now."

Lin didn't know what to say in response to the compliment, or how to take the implication that she was to be part of his life, for that was impossible.

"May I put it on you?" Gideon asked, gesturing at the necklace.

Lin nodded, then unhooked it from the little clasps that had held it in its bed of blue silk.

She offered it to Gideon. "Here."

"Turn around," he instructed, and she obediently turned her back to him.

He reached over her and first opened her collar a bit more. Lin briefly closed her eyes, again overwhelmed by the touch of a new man. A man she desired.

He settled the necklace against her skin. Lin held the

pendant in place and tipped her head downward while he worked the chain's tiny fastening. She wondered if he, too, could feel the pulse fluttering at her neck, just like the swallows' wings on his wonderful gift to her.

"There," he said, then stepped back in front of her.

"Thank you," she repeated, and smiled up at him.

It seemed that time stilled around them. Lin knew she should move, should do something to break the spell that held them, but she was too curious to see what might happen next.

Gideon moved a step closer. His strong, warm hand drifted across the skin of her cheek and then briefly touched her hair, where it was pulled back from her temple.

She felt herself swaying toward him. They were going to kiss. She knew this and wanted it, yet feared it, too. Feared it enough that she needed to delay the moment. She drew slightly away, and to distract him, seized on the first topic that entered her mind.

"Have you…have you heard anything about Ariana?"

He hesitated, no doubt trying to mentally wend his way to her new line of conversation. "Ariana Bennett?"

"Yes. The librarian who showed me the Chinese antiquities book. The woman who went missing?"

She watched as he turned from man and potential lover back into ship's officer. Cold water in the face couldn't have worked any better than her question.

"I know who Miss Bennett is. I simply hadn't expected to hear her name right *now*."

Lin clasped her hands together so that she would not flutter them about. "Yes, well..."

"We did absolutely everything we could regarding Miss Bennett," he said.

What she'd meant as a detour became her focus. "Which is exactly the same thing we were all told the day after she didn't come back. Is there no more you can do to locate her after all this time when no one has heard from her?"

"My powers are limited. All I can do is file a missing persons report, which I did, and ask the home office to follow up to the degree possible...which I also did."

"I don't understand.... And so she just disappears forever?"

He shoved his hand through his sandy brown hair in a gesture of impatience. "Lin, most every employee who leaves in the middle of a cruise does so because they are no longer able to handle life on the ship."

"But Ariana was very comfortable here. She had her friends...many of them—"

"And I've heard from them all, including you. We have responded the best that we can."

"I believe you're giving this... What's that phrase?" She searched her mind for the bit of idiom that seemed to have hidden away. "Ah! You give this matter lip service!"

She'd no sooner spoken than it struck her: *lip service*. She'd talked herself right back to the very spot she'd intended to avoid.

Her gaze fixed on his mouth. It was a very fine

mouth, broad and masculine, neither too thin-lipped nor too full. It was a mouth deserving of...*lip service*.

Lin gave up the game. She watched his gray, thickly lashed eyes grow wide with surprise as she came to him and then brushed her lips once, twice against his.

Just to get the feel of him, she thought, but knew herself for a liar. She wanted more than the feel. She wanted the taste. She wanted—

Gideon pulled her closer, closed his mouth over hers, then backed her until she was leaning against the side wall of her tiny room. She twined her arms around him, pressing her body to his. It was heaven, feeling a man— no, *this man*—against her, after so very much loneliness.

His tongue touched her lower lip...a brief foray, as though he asked for permission before exploring more. Lin opened her mouth wider, moving closer, wanting to absorb his essence into her. They kissed for long, sweet minutes, mouths meeting, moving, matching at new angles as they learned the taste and feel of each other.

Gasping, Gideon pulled away. "I need to see your hair down. Please..."

Hands trembling, Lin unpinned it, then shook it out, letting it settle in its usual sleek lines about her shoulders.

"Beautiful," he said, and she knew that he meant more than just her hair.

This time, he came to her, and their kisses grew hotter, so hot that she wanted to give herself to him, right there in her place of work, not caring that a client was soon due.

"I can't bear this," she said. "I need to see your skin, feel you…"

He groaned, then let his mouth travel downward, trailing kisses down her neck. She pushed her hips against him, wanting more…starving for more. He tugged down the collar of her shirt, kissing first the necklace he'd given her, then nipping at her collarbone. Lin gasped her pleasure. She'd always been so sensitive there. He murmured something, but she wasn't sure what, for it hadn't been in their common English.

She felt the press of his tongue hot against her skin, and she cried out, release nearly on her. Her heart pounded and her breasts tingled. There was not enough air in the room….

And then she felt something that usually only occurred when she held her child to her. Lin froze as her milk began to let down.

"Stop!" she cried, placing her hands on Gideon's shoulders and pushing him back.

"Why?" he asked, his tone deep and ragged. "Am I not giving you pleasure?"

If only he could know how much…

She crossed her arms over her chest. In an instant, if not already, the milk would be seeping through her clothing.

Gideon turned his back to her. Hands on hips and head down, he dragged in a breath.

"I am sorry," he said. "I lost…lost—"

She could not let him feel responsible for her necessary deception.

"No," Lin said. "It's me. Just me, and nothing you've done. If you could just…just…"

What could she do? It wasn't as though she could explain to this man that she just happened to have a son whom she'd begun to quickly wean to the bottle today, and ever-so-sorry if she seemed to be leaking.

He turned back to face her. "Let's not do this. Let's not stumble over words and hurt each other. We both need to gather our thoughts. May I see you tonight? After dinner, will you walk with me…the Helios deck at, say, nine?"

If she was not mistaken, Gideon Dayan had just asked her out on a date. They were taking events a bit backward considering what they'd just been doing, but she was charmed all the same. Lin gave him the only answer possible.

"Yes."

CHAPTER EIGHT

LIN STOOD JUST INSIDE the main doorway that led from the spa area to the Helios deck's many outside offerings. Earlier, she had skipped dinner, eating only a bit of fruit, then nursing Wei just enough to ease some of the pressure she felt and some of the frustration that had him waving his arms about and screwing his little face into a pucker. Before leaving him in Zhang's care, she had apologized to him for what they were both going through, and promised him a very long cuddle tonight.

Nervous in a way that seemed almost silly for a twenty-six-year-old widow and mother of one, Lin touched her fingers to the pendant that Gideon had given her, seeking calm. She had arrived at their designated meeting point several minutes early for that very same reason.

"Lin? Lin, is that really you?"

Lin turned and smiled at Mrs. Saperstein, a woman who had been a frequent client on this cruise.

"Hello, Mrs. Saperstein."

The older woman took Lin's hand in her own and patted it. "Hello, yourself. You look gorgeous, dear! Now give me a spin and show that dress off."

Lin obliged, executing a twirl that sent the skirt of

her red silk dress belling outward. The sleeveless cocktail dress with its almost daring scooped neck was the only good dress Lin owned. It also set off Gideon's pendant as the piece deserved.

"Stunning," Mrs. Saperstein declared. "Like a Chinese Audrey Hepburn!"

Lin laughed. She knew she looked nice in the dress, but to be compared to Audrey Hepburn, whose movies Lin had watched during her lonely nights in Hong Kong?

"Mrs. Saperstein, you are too kind."

"No, honey, I'm just honest." She glanced over Lin's shoulder. "And I think I see someone else who thinks you're looking red-hot."

Gideon must have arrived! Smiling, Lin turned.

Instead of Gideon standing there, she saw Dima Ivanov. He must have just come from work, as he was still dressed in his fitness centre uniform of track pants and white T-shirt with the ship's insignia.

Lin's smile disappeared.

Not quite sure what else to do, she turned back to Mrs. Saperstein, but the older woman wasn't going to serve as a good buffer.

"Well, I'll let you get on with your night, lovey," she said to Lin. "Ah, to be young again!"

At that very moment, Lin was finding youth to be of no great merit. If she could move time forward until she was off this ship and her world had righted itself, she'd be just fine with that. Except for missing out on her time with Gideon... As Dima approached, her hand rose to the pendant and rested there.

"You're all dressed up," he said, his usually jovial features in a downturn.

"I am," Lin agreed.

She knew that Dima was angry. She owed him no apology, but if it would smooth the waters—so to speak—she would offer one, anyway.

"Dima, I want to—"

"Is that what he gave you?" he interrupted.

"What?"

He pointed at the necklace. "That. Did Dayan give you that?"

Lin stood silent.

Ivanov snorted. "So say nothing. It was all over the ship today."

"What do you mean?"

"Helga saw him carry a gift back to you, and now you wear this."

He flicked a hand toward the pendant, where it rested just above the neckline of her dress. If Lin hadn't moved back, he would have made contact with her.

"You made me think you wanted me, and all along you were with him. He buys you. Like a whore, he buys you."

Though Dima Ivanov couldn't have been further from the truth, the anger in his blow still struck home.

Lin gasped. "How can you—"

His look was one of pure hatred. "Say nothing. I now know what you are."

Dima turned and left.

She had made another enemy in a world that already

held so many for her. Her pleasure in the evening began to seep away, but then she remembered what Gideon had told her. She was giving the Russian too much power, once again. There was nothing he could do to hurt her, and it would be his gain if she permitted him to tarnish her night.

After taking a moment to regain her emotional footing, Lin made her way outside, but lingered near the doors so Gideon could find her. The weather off the Turkish coast remained kissed with warmth in late September, yet Lin felt a chill.

She heard the soft *swish* of the doors opening. Gideon approached, and her heart eased.

"Lin?" he said as he neared. "I'm sorry to be late. I was delayed by a slight matter."

He wore his white dress uniform, which only gave a deeper golden cast to his skin. She'd always heard the other women aboard ship talking about how handsome he was, but she hadn't seen it...until lately. Perhaps her eyes had still been clouded by grief.

"I'm just happy you're here, now," Lin replied, rubbing her arms to chase off the last of the cold that Ivanov's words had brought.

"Are you cold?" Gideon asked, one hand going to the buttons on his jacket. "Would you like to use this?"

"No, thank you. I'm fine, really...just adjusting to the breeze," she fibbed.

She wished that he could hold her and help her forget the venom of Dima's verbal attack. But it was enough of a bending of propriety that he would walk with her among the cruise passengers. She would not ask for more.

"Shall we?" he asked, gesturing at the expanse of deck.

"Yes."

Twilight was giving way to night. A thin crescent of moon shone low in the cloudless sky, in which the stars were just beginning to wake. Many were enjoying the beauty. Some couples stood together at the rail. Others sat on the benches that were tucked here and there for the passengers' relaxation.

By unspoken agreement, Lin and Gideon began to stroll along the outside of the deck. They stood close to each other, but did not touch. Still, Lin could feel the same magnetism that connected the other couples on the deck drawing her to this man. At first, they talked of nothing more pressing than the beauty of the night. But Lin knew there were things to be said, and that it would do her no good to wait.

"I do desire you," she blurted.

Gideon paused in his walking, so Lin stopped, too.

"I noticed," he said. "Just as I'm sure you noticed that I desire you."

She nodded.

He took her hands in his. "What we do with this desire is up to you. No matter how it seemed this morning, you need to know that I will never push you…never give more than you want."

"I know that…. I do." And when the time was right, she would ask for it all. "This is new to me."

He chuckled. "And to me, too."

It didn't seem that way to Lin, but perhaps she was so awash in her own concerns, she hadn't noticed his.

"Let's walk," he said, then companionably settled her hand so that it rested in the crook of his bent elbow.

The breeze, which had been settling for the night, briefly roused. Lin lifted her face into it, savoring the clean, salt-kissed scent in the air.

"So, you were married," Gideon stated more than asked.

"Yes," Lin replied.

"And then you lost him?"

"I did."

She fell into silence, and Gideon did not urge her on. She appreciated his patience.

"This is difficult for me," she eventually said. "My husband was a man facing enormous challenges. For my safety, we paid some bribe money and married in a rural province far from where we lived. We kept our marriage a secret from many. Even now, I am not accustomed to speaking of him to one who did not know him."

"Then tell me about him, though I already know one thing about him, for certain."

"And that is?"

"He was very lucky to be married to you."

She ducked her head so that under the deck's perimeter lights he could not see the warm color blossoming on her cheeks.

"Thank you," she said.

"You don't need to thank me for speaking the truth."

Lin thanked him again, earning a laugh and a smile. Then she gathered her thoughts and began in earnest.

"I met Wei while in Beijing, where I was both studying and teaching English to others. The first time I saw him, I knew that my life had just changed. I was so startled that I turned and fled, leaving his cousin to apologize for my odd behavior."

She didn't add that the second time in her life that she'd felt such an intense sense of recognition had been with Gideon.

"Wei persevered, then?" Gideon asked.

Lin smiled at the memory. "He did. I ended up volunteering to help him with letters in English translation for his human rights group."

Gideon's pace slowed. "He was an activist, then?"

"Yes," she said proudly. "He grew up in a village with much pollution, and by the time he was fifteen, he was helping organize workers in the battery plant to protest the fact that they were forced to contaminate their own land and thus poison their children. He did such a good job that his parents sent him off to live with cousins until Wei was old enough to start university."

"Industrious boy," Gideon said.

Lin laughed. "Who grew into a driven man. Wei angered many. We had the authorities seize our belongings so many times that I learned to hide my clothing and favored possessions at friends' apartments…all the better to hide our marriage from those in Beijing, anyway."

"It must have been a challenging life."

"It was a worthy life, and my time with him was too short."

"What happened?" he asked.

Lin stopped walking and put herself back in that dark place that had been her life. As she began to speak, the horrible tension of those days again coursed through her body.

"The pressure on Wei was growing. He knew he was being watched round the clock. He made me move in with friends so that I would be safer.

"I begged him to let someone else take the lead for a while…just until the authorities reduced their scrutiny, since he was no help to anyone with all the eyes upon him. Wei agreed. We made plans to visit Paris, but he could not get permission to leave the country. This angered him."

Lin had never seen Wei like that, so furious that he could focus on nothing else. He hadn't made love to her in weeks, but she'd been accepting of that, because she'd been feeling sick with tension, too. At least, that's what she'd thought was unsettling her stomach….

"He decided to lead a protest to commemorate those who lost their lives years ago at Tiananmen Square, fighting for the same freedoms he sought," she told Gideon. "He marched there, and in the melee that followed, over a dozen students died. Wei escaped, but they picked him up a day later. They kept him for thirteen days."

Lin had been able to do nothing but wait. She'd

gone about her life as always—teaching and studying and trying to pretend that her heart hadn't been ripped from her.

"Thirteen days doesn't sound so long a time, does it?" she asked Gideon.

He didn't answer.

"The man who came home was not the man they had taken," she said. "He was ill…so very ill, and it wasn't just from what they'd done to persuade him to give the names of his group's other leaders, both in China and abroad."

"I'm sorry that both of you suffered so," Gideon said.

"I wanted to take him to the hospital, but he told me that it would do no good. One way or another, in the state's hands, they would kill him. He felt he was safer trying to recover in our apartment, with me. His hair fell out. He could keep no food down, and then he started vomiting his own blood. There was nothing anyone could do."

Wei Chan had died in her arms. His death had been neither romantic nor peaceful. It had been horrible, and it was all she could do to keep the memory locked away in its little box.

She gripped the ship's railing and looked out to sea. "They poisoned him. I am as sure of that as I am of my own name. They poisoned him and sent him home as a message to others in the group that this would be their fate, too."

"And so you left?"

Lin nodded. "I moved to Hong Kong and trained in therapeutic massage. I liked the idea of learning a skill that could be used anywhere. Then, when word came to me that the Beijing authorities wanted to question me about what I might know of the group, I knew I needed to be farther away. I took the job on *Alexandra's Dream* before Beijing could put a hold on my passport. I had seen what had happened to my husband."

What she did not—could not—add was that as much as she had feared for herself, she had feared a hundredfold for the small life growing inside her. First, the child was to be cared for. Only after that could she assure that Wei Chan's death carried meaning…that as he watched over her, he knew it had not been fully in vain.

She glanced at Gideon. He, too, was watching the roll and swell of the sea.

"Surely Wei Chan knew that he and others might die if he chose to march on Tiananmen?" he asked without turning his gaze to her.

"Yes."

"And you didn't find this extreme?"

"Sometimes life requires extreme measures," she said, thinking of her son now belowdecks with Zhang.

"And sometimes less extreme measures would work just as well."

Why was this man beginning to argue with her?

"Wei had considered all of this. The anniversary of Tiananmen was one of the few times he thought that he might be able to get clear word to the outside world. You know that my government has killed many, Gideon. Most you never hear of. It's as though there are so many of my people that we are not valued as individuals, but all leave behind families who mourn."

"My point, exactly."

She did not understand the bitterness in his voice. "Why do you attack his choices?"

"Why do *you* defend them?"

"Because I loved him, and I knew what he was when I fell in love with him." Her voice was rising to meet his anger. Lin paused until she could calm herself. "And because I believe in his cause."

He muttered something she didn't quite catch.

"What?"

He turned to her and ran his finger around the circle of jade that rested warm against her skin.

"Nothing," he said. "Nothing at all."

"It didn't sound like nothing. But in the interest of peace, let's let it go."

Gideon shook his head. "Beautiful and a diplomat, too. I'm sorry I'm such poor company." He pushed back his cuff and glanced at his watch. "It's getting late. We both should get some sleep."

Lin knew it wasn't all that late, but she also knew that something had upset Gideon Dayan. He looked as though a ghost had danced across his vision.

She was sorting through what to say next when he took her hand and placed a kiss on the back of it.

"We're quite a complicated pair, aren't we?" he asked. "But I like you, Lin. Very much. By the time we're through tiptoeing around each other, we'll be spoiled for anyone else."

Lin suspected she already was.

THE DIGITS ON Gideon's clock shone a bright green 1:47. At least he had managed to sleep a few hours— quite a feat considering what Lin had told him.

Once, after an adolescent friend of Gideon's had died, his mother had tried to comfort him by saying that everything happens for a reason. He had found the words hollow at the time—just a fruitless effort to superimpose the comfort of order over a random and chaotic world.

But to meet Lin and find that she had been widowed in such a way? God might remain inscrutable, but perhaps there was a pattern to His works, after all. Lin's situation resonated all too clearly with his. Yet if they had been brought together to find peace, they were doing a miserably poor job of it.

Gideon closed his eyes. One last time he would permit himself to think of the day that ended his idea of Forever. One last time, and then he and Rachel would let each other go.

Eilat, Israel—sixteen months earlier

"ARE YOU EVER GOING to come out of that bathroom?" Gideon called through the closed door. "You don't need a full face of makeup to go scuba diving."

"But I did need to shave my legs," Rachel replied as

she swung open the door and came out, beach bag slung over her shoulder.

"They seemed pretty smooth when you had them wrapped around my back earlier," Gideon said.

She laughed. "As if you'd have noticed. You were concentrating on other parts of your body."

She had him on that.

"Ready to go?" he asked.

"Always."

He swung her into his arms. "Still love me?"

She laughed. "Always."

EILAT HAD TAKEN ON the atmosphere of a street festival. Though the march was not until the next day, students congregated along the beach and in front of every café in town. The military had made their initial showing in order to supplement the local police, and yesterday, Gideon and Rachel had met with the core team of officials in charge of keeping the peace. Nothing untoward was expected, but all the same, Gideon had been feeling tense. Last night, he'd scarcely slept, when usually he slept like the dead.

Gear bags slung over their backs, he and Rachel wove through the crowd and down the seaside walk to the dive shop.

"It's all one big party," Rachel said to him over the noise of students dancing to the driving beat of techno music blaring from a radio. "Too big. Fools…"

Gideon considered what she said and wondered if she had the same sense of discomfort that had seized him. Though they were far from the country's hot zones, the march tomorrow would be a rich target, richer than a border crossing, a market, a nightclub, or any of the usual terrorism locales. At this point, though, there was nothing he could do.

"This party isn't as big as the one in our bed this morning," he said teasingly to Rachel in an effort to keep their moods light. "Too bad I wore you out."

"We'll see who goes first tonight," she said, the glint of challenge bright in her brown eyes.

"You're on." This was one aspect of her competitive nature that he enjoyed down to the soles of his feet.

The covered area where the divers assembled their gear was as packed as the rest of the seaside. Rachel and Gideon managed to stake a claim at the end of one bench just inside the shelter's entryway.

"Looks like it's going to be one of those follow-the-leader dives," Rachel said. "I should have asked how many others were booked."

"You'll love it all the same once we're down there," Gideon replied as he checked out his regulator.

When he looked up, they were there again—the young couple. He was wearing bathing trunks and a short-sleeved shirt, ready to go for a dive. The girl must have just accompanied him to see him off. She wore a flowing skirt and a loose, long-sleeved gauzy black top.

They edged into the shelter. Since no space on the benches remained, the young man set his dive bag on the ground and looked around as though seeking the dive master. He seemed to have a case of neophyte's nerves.

"First time?" Gideon asked in Hebrew, and got no response. He tried again in Arabic, but the man's attention had wandered elsewhere. His lover was clasping his elbow and tugging at him, as though she didn't intend to let him go.

Sweet, he thought. Until he noticed her tears.

The fine hairs on the back of Gideon's neck stood up. He might be slow in taking the clues God sent his way, but he wasn't hopelessly stupid. He glanced over at Rachel, who sat next to him on the bench. She, too, was watching the couple.

"Not good," Gideon murmured to her.

She nodded her head in agreement.

The younger man whispered something to the girl, then in a very calm voice said aloud, *"Allahu akbar."*

Gideon knew these Arabic words of prayer and praise well. He also knew that sometimes they were a harbinger of ill to come.

"Allahu akbar," the girl repeated with no calm at all. She gave her lover a wild-eyed look and wheeled toward the shelter's exit.

One word had etched itself in Gideon's mind: *bomb.*

It was a day too damn early, and not at the protest march, but wouldn't that make some sense? Security was lax. Damn it, he'd been lax.

The gear bag!

Acting on instinct, he threw himself on top of the man's blue duffel....

And...

Absolutely bloody nothing happened.

Except for a few peals of nervous laughter, the shelter fell silent.

Gideon tried to come up with a decent excuse for his insanity, even though virtually everyone in there must have guessed what he'd been thinking.

"I…ah…"

From his belly-down position on the concrete, a slight movement caught his eye. The girl was nervously shifting her weight from one sandal-clad foot to the other. Her hand hovered near her waist, which was covered by folds of fabric from the loose tuniclike shirt.

"Shit!" He'd chosen wrong.

He leaped to his feet, but someone was in front of him.

"Mine," Rachel said.

She flew at the girl, wrapped her arms around her and sent them both slamming out of the shelter and onto the emptier walk.

His cry of terror and fury was swallowed by searing heat and a force he'd never felt before. And then, he, too, was swallowed by the force and brought into a world of blackness….

And when he came out of the blackness a few days later, the doctors confirmed what he'd already known. Rachel Shalev had exited his life just as she'd entered it…with no holds barred.

"SO DAMN COMPETITIVE that you had to die first, too, didn't you?" Gideon asked the presence that had been with him since that day. "It was supposed to have been my damn turn."

He knew what she'd say, even though she wasn't there to say it: *"Then you shouldn't have chosen wrong, lover."*

He'd blamed her for her self-sacrifice for months, and he continued to blame himself for screwing up. But the truth was that the blame rested with those who believed in carnage as a way to deliver a message and those foolhardy enough to intentionally put themselves in harm's way.

He had lost his lover in the protection of fools.

CHAPTER NINE

"REMIND ME WHY I don't usually go ashore in Antalya," Zhang said the following noon after entering Lin's cabin.

Lin adjusted her grip on the bottle she was giving Wei. This morning he'd kindly decided to take one from her without first rooting at her breast in search of the real thing, then bemoaning his mother's cruelty for failing him so.

"Could it be the twenty-five miles each way on the bus to the city?" Lin asked.

"Exactly. But it's good that I took the trip."

"You heard from your contacts, then?" As Zhang had expected, there had been no return e-mail from China while they'd been in Bodrum.

Zhang nodded. "I have news, though it's not the news I'd like to give you. It has been confirmed first-hand…. Wei Chan's parents know about baby Wei."

Lin looked down at her child, so innocent and so unaware of the turmoil around him. If only she could shelter him completely. It wasn't until a tear hit his face and he flinched that she even realized she was crying.

"How could this happen?" she whispered to herself, but Zhang took the rhetorical question quite literally.

"You know how well connected they are, and with money enough to fill any hungry palm."

From what their son had once told Lin, Ji and Quio Chan were the richest in their village, and perhaps their region. It wasn't until Wei had grown older that he had understood how his family afforded the only brick home, the finest car and two servants. As the officials in charge of business licenses for the area, his parents had discovered that turning a blind eye to certain improprieties could line their pockets. They had turned that blind eye often. Ultimately, they had also turned out Wei Chan, whose personal beliefs did not mesh with their kickback scheme.

"It could be worse," Lin said. "They're in China, and I have just over a week until I leave the ship."

"And it might not be that easy. Lin, they've left the village to travel, but they were very vague on where. I know I'm the one who tells you not to worry, but I think that now a little worry would be a very prudent thing."

"Then I'm already the most prudent person on earth," she replied.

Wei had reached the end of his bottle. Lin set it aside. Using a hand towel to protect her uniform, she settled her son against her shoulder for a good burp. It was a basic act, one she'd done countless times in his brief life, but it was just what she needed to stem her panic. The steady rise and fall of his little chest reminded her that this was how she should proceed: one breath at a time.

She could not control Wei Chan's parents or change their desires, whatever those might be. They had sent off their own son before he was sixteen. They had not claimed Wei's body after his death. Why should they have any interest in his son? With so many unknowns, the best that she could do was prepare herself, should these shadow adversaries arrive.

"Let's assume they're looking for me," Lin said. "There's no evidence to lead them here."

Zhang hesitated before speaking. "No, there's not, except that Tao's e-mail worries me."

"But you said that she does not know that I am here."

"She *did* not, but if Wei Chan's parents learned of this and Quio Chan then told her sister, Tao's mother…" She trailed off, then shook her head. "It's all speculation, and Tao would never answer me directly. Her job at the battery factory depends on staying in Quio Chan's good graces."

Wei let loose a content baby belch, and both the women laughed.

Breath by breath and heartbeat by heartbeat, Lin thought. That was how she'd see herself through the coming days.

AS FAR AS GIDEON was concerned, Lin Wang worked far too hard. However, he had the good sense not to share his opinion on the topic with her. She'd simply tell him that she was strong enough to handle it, and she'd no doubt be right. Still, just the thought of the hours he'd witnessed her keeping on this shorthanded cruise tired him out. Helga the guardian had long ago left her spa desk, the aestheticians had all gone on their way, but even though it was past nine at night Lin still labored in her massage room.

Gideon had a dozen other places he could—and some that he should—be. But he owed Lin an explanation for his reaction last night, and until he'd accomplished that, all else must wait.

Patience eventually paid off. Lin arrived in the reception area, along with an older woman.

He felt his smile grow as Lin noticed him. He loved the shy way she ducked her head, especially because he knew that when alone, shyness was not necessarily an issue. Assuming he ever had the opportunity to be alone with her again...

Lin neared. She still wore his necklace. Gideon took that as a good sign.

He greeted her with a hello and then waited for her to finish up with her client.

"So is he your next customer?" the woman asked, giving Gideon a once-over that both amused and marginally embarrassed him. "If so, your job has some *real* benefits."

Lin smiled. "No more than getting to talk to you, Mrs. Saperstein."

"Hah! I was young once, too, you know." She dug into her purse and pressed some money on Lin. "A little extra since you stayed so late for me," she stage-whispered.

Lin thanked the woman, who gave Gideon a saucy wink before ambling off to the bank of elevators.

"Are you finished for the evening?" Gideon asked.

"Finally," Lin said. "My hands are numb. One more massage and they would have fallen off."

"I think, then, that it's your turn to be pampered."

She blinked. "My turn?"

He took her by the hand. "Back to your room, Miss Wang."

She dug in her sneaker-clad heels. "I really can't."

Gideon turned her hand over. In deep, steady strokes, he rubbed his thumb across the soft skin of her palm.

Head tipped back, Lin sighed her pleasure. "That's wonderful, but I promised a friend that I'd help her...."

He switched to her other hand and said, "Just imagine what I can do for your back."

Their eyes met. He could see that she fought some sort of internal battle he didn't understand. He stopped his ministrations and kissed the inside of her palm.

"Please?" he asked. "We both could use the time alone."

"Maybe for a few minutes," she said.

Gideon would take what he could get.

Lin escorted him back to the massage room. He watched as she expertly stripped the table and refreshed the sheets with new linens from a cupboard. When she was done, he dimmed the lights.

"Take off as little or as much clothing as makes you feel comfortable," he instructed, echoing the words she gave him prior to every massage.

She smiled. "And you will wait outside a few moments until I am ready?"

"Yes, if you insist." He knew he sounded like a child asking if he must eat all of his peas, and wasn't surprised when she laughed.

"No, stay."

Now, that surprised him.

Lin turned her back and quickly peeled off her white uniform polo shirt. Any small hope Gideon had carried for a sensual striptease perished at that moment. Without once showing him any more than her slender white back, she got onto the table and stretched out.

"No oils," she said briskly. "I must wear these pants again tomorrow and want no stains."

"You could always take them off," he suggested.

"And you can get about your business, Gideon Dayan," she said without so much as picking up her head from where it rested in the table's cradle. "You promised me a massage."

So he had. And it was a good thing she'd taken this all-business tone with him, since he'd nearly forgotten his first intention…that of talk, not touch.

Ah, but to touch… He rubbed his hands together, making sure they were warm enough not to startle her. He started by rubbing the base of her skull in a circular motion with his fingertips, easing the tension out. Gideon smiled as she began to relax further into the table.

"Am I doing well?" he asked.

"For an amateur."

He could hear the smile in her voice. He traced her necklace's chain, where it rested in that vulnerable spot at the bottom of her neck. She shivered, and he felt his body respond. For a while, he worked on her shoulders, knowing that he'd found a spot especially in need of attention by the low purr that Lin gave.

Gideon began to work his way down. Her practical white bra—nothing flirtatious or frilly about it—crossed her back like a roadway barrier. He settled his hand over the closure.

"May I?" he asked. At her nodded assent, he unhooked the bra, smoothed it out of his way and let his hand travel unimpeded down the sleek length of her back. He imagined letting his mouth follow the same course…tasting her ivory skin, feeling her warmth beneath his lips. But before that—and so much more—could be real, there were other barriers that needed to fall, too.

Gideon had thought long and hard about what to tell Lin. He'd balanced what she needed to know against the sure knowledge that, in telling her, his anger at the past would rise again. He had let go of the idea that living with memories of Rachel would be enough for him. But still the anger burned.

He ran the heels of his hands down either side of Lin's spine. He loved it when she did that to him, and hoped it brought her the same kind of pleasure.

"You have seen my scars," he finally said as he worked.

She nodded. "And felt them, too."

"Why I carry them has much to do with my reaction to what you told me about your husband last night."

"I wondered as much, when I thought about you today. Will you tell me what happened?"

"You had Wei, your husband, and once I had Rachel, my lover. We were coworkers, both with the Mossad, the secret service in my homeland."

"I had heard it whispered that you were once with them."

"I still am. I've taken a leave until I'm physically ready to go back." Gideon wasn't sure why he'd added that, except that it was so much a part of how he saw himself, and he wanted her to understand just how much he had lost. It wasn't just Rachel, but his sense of who he was in the world, and what his destiny was meant to be.

"Rachel and I were sent to assist in security measures to protect a student march. The students were angered over our country's pullout from Gaza and the West Bank. They believed that the Palestinian Authority was going to send some of their higher-ups to a symposium on Arab-Israeli relations that was being held in Eilat…a resort city in Israel's south."

"A symposium with press coverage?" Lin said. "The perfect place for a protest, then."

"In theory," Gideon replied. "There were two problems. First, the Palestinian Authority had never planned on sending anyone. Beyond that, this protest idea took on a life of its own. With that came the concern that the students might be attracting too much attention. We spoke with the student leaders about the risks inherent in assembling a group of that size, and how their actions were going to make an already diffi-cult situation more dangerous for those they inflamed. They didn't believe us, of course."

"Or perhaps they chose to assume that risk?" Lin asked.

Gideon felt his hands tighten with frustration. He took care not to let that translate into his touch on Lin's back.

"Some risks one should only assume for oneself. Rachel and I, we knew that our job came with a good measure of personal danger. We accepted that and we lived accordingly. These students…it was different, Lin. Some were caught up in the fervor of the moment, but some clearly thought of this as a holiday…some fun marching for a cause…."

Gideon shook his head. "God, how I hate that word, *cause*…."

"Why?" Lin asked. "It's a noble concept."

"Only as noble as the acts carried out in its name are pure," he replied. "The day before the march, Rachel and I were going to take a short scuba diving tour. The staging area for equipment checks and the like was just off a crowded walk. And I do mean crowded. Imagine the crowd that disembarks from *Alexandra's Dream* when we come into port, then multiply it fivefold."

Lin gave a slight nod of her head.

"Rachel and I were getting ready for our dive when a young couple I'd seen here and there arrived, too. Something about them had already gained my attention. They were tense and arguing when most everyone else among the students seemed to be having fun. This day, the girl was acting oddly. Both Rachel and I knew something was about to happen, and because history tends to repeat itself in my world, I suspected they carried a bomb.

"I bet that the man had it in his dive bag. As it turned out, I was wrong. The girl had the bomb. Rachel dragged her down and took the brunt of the blow. She died instantly. I came away with what you have seen on me."

"And what you carry in your heart," Lin added after a moment's silence. "Those scars, I'm sure, are more painful than what I have seen."

His hands stilled, and he bent to place a kiss on her back.

"You're a perceptive woman," he said, leaving one hand settled above the waistline of her white pants, just because he felt better when touching her.

"And so when will you go back home?" she asked him.

"I'm not sure. I think, sometimes, that I have seen and felt enough. I've devoted nearly fifteen years of my life to the military and to the Mossad. After these months on ship, I still wake some mornings and I find myself tired...not physically, but mentally. It's growing harder and harder to remain a warrior...to keep the edge that would keep me alive and save others. With Rachel and the seven others who died in that blast, I failed."

"I'm sorry for your loss. I know how deeply the pain cuts."

He was sure that she did, which was one of the reasons he could speak to her of this when he spoke to so few others.

"All the same, I do not understand how the manner of Wei's death could have angered you so."

"It wasn't how he died, it was that he brought others along with him. Lin, there are those who choose to be involved in political issues, and those who charm or coerce others into situations they're not equipped to handle.... Your Wei, he measured the risks and then inflamed others to move on heedlessly."

She propped herself up on her arms and turned her head to the side so that their eyes met.

"You can't know that," she said, her voice flat. "And you can't apply what happened to you to situations in a part of the world you know little about. And if he did bring others to their deaths, that is a burden that the leader of a cause must assume."

"*Cause!* That word again. I hear that word and I think of senseless bloodshed. Martyrs with their causes are the most dangerous people on earth. I risked my life for such a martyr, and Rachel died covering one."

"I am sorry. Truly, I am. But some freedoms are worth any cost."

"And you are the judge of which freedoms and the means to be used to get them?" he asked.

"In my own land and with my own life, I am."

How could he make her see what he had? How could he give her his life lessons without sounding as much a zealot as some of those martyrs?

She gave him no chance. "I plan to take up Wei's work as soon as I'm resettled. I will be leaving my job here at the end of the next cruise, and moving at least temporarily to live with friends in France. This place was never more than a safe harbor until I can take the steps that are required of me."

He'd had no idea she was leaving, but that news was secondary to the bloody theme he heard playing out in her intentions. "*Required* of you? Who is requiring this?"

"Honor…both my own and that of Wei's memory."

More martyr talk. In his experience, those who spoke of higher ideals had not often considered the base practicalities.

"And how do you plan to take these required steps?" he asked, trying to keep his frustration from showing in his tone.

"Eventually I will return to China…but under my own plan, and not because the government has compelled me."

"Plan? You will return, and then what?"

"I will take off where Wei Chan left off. I will organize protests and I will work to see that a few no longer get rich off the lives of many."

Chan… That was the first time she'd given him her late husband's surname. Gideon mentally filed it away, then thought again about what she'd just said.

"Wait… You told me that your husband died at the hands of the Beijing authorities, correct?"

"Yes."

"And yet you plan to go back there?"

"Of course. There is much work to be done. You take your freedom for granted, Gideon."

"After what I've been through, I take *nothing* for

granted. But you—your intentions are incredibly dangerous...and horribly naive, too. What makes you think you'll fare any better than your husband did?"

She shifted uncomfortably on the massage table. "Wait. I cannot talk to you like this. Turn your back."

"Fine." He was angry and frustrated enough that he half wanted not only to turn his back, but to walk from this room and leave Mei Lin Wang alone on her inevitable march to martyrdom. But perhaps he was growing to be a martyr in his own small way, and she was his cause. So he stayed and schooled himself to patience.

"You may turn around, now." She had rehooked her bra and wrapped the table's sheet around her like a woman might a towel when coming from the shower. "You asked why I might fare better? My experience of having seen his mistakes will guide me. At times, Wei let temper rule him—"

"Where you're letting a blind addiction to nobility rule you. What is the difference?"

She sighed. "You cannot understand this."

"And you cannot have thought this through fully. You're a smart and perceptive person, Lin. Please...for your own sake...promise me that you will make no rash decisions."

One hand holding her makeshift top in place, she slipped from the table and stood. Back to him again, she dropped the sheet and pulled on her shirt.

"Can we not agree to disagree on philosophical matters and simply enjoy our time together?" she asked once she'd turned back around.

He smiled in spite of himself. "Isn't that a question that the man usually asks?"

Her lips briefly curved upward. "Perhaps, but in this instance it's the question a very practical woman is asking."

The room's phone began to ring.

"Annoying beast," she said.

Gideon could only hope that she referred to the telephone.

Lin lifted the receiver. "Hello?"

Gideon watched as she started with surprise, then glanced at her watch. "That late already! I am so sorry. I'll be right there."

She hung up and returned her attention to Gideon. "I must leave now. Friends have been waiting for me. But first…"

She neared, and despite the utter frustration he felt over her blind adherence to ideals, Gideon's heart beat faster. He was a man, even if an angry one.

She came up on tiptoe and placed a kiss on his mouth.

"Please think about what I offer," she said. Her hands still lingered at his shoulders, and his body began to harden in response. "No promises past port in Piraeus at the end of next week, but until then…"

Passion.

Gideon craved it as much as he did his next breath, but could he watch yet another woman he cared for become a ghost in his life? Yes, he was a man, but he wasn't certain that he was that strong.

CHAPTER TEN

THE MEDIEVAL WALLS surrounding the Old City of Rhodes hid a maze that rivaled Lin's knotted thoughts the following morning. Since the port was within walking distance of all one could need, both she and Zhang had decided to steal away for a short shopping excursion for necessaries.

As she and her friend crossed under St. Catherine's Gate and into the Old City proper, they made their plans. Zhang needed an Internet café since she was not in a position to move about as freely as Lin when on the ship. Wei required some more powdered formula and a new pacifier, since his had gone missing sometime yesterday evening before Lin had returned to her cabin. Zhang, Awa and Cambro had retraced their steps, but to no avail. Wei was becoming one unhappy little warrior.

Lin's search was more personal in nature. She sought everything necessary to seduce a man. She was accepting of her own charms. Her body was nice enough that many men looked twice, and her hair remained her secret pride. But she suspected it would take more than that to persuade Gideon Dayan past his differences with her. She was a stubborn woman, and knew a stubborn man when she met one.

The September sky was a vivid blue overhead, with none of the hints of showers that sometimes visited Rhodes in the autumn, and the breeze remained warm and dry. Lin entered a small shop that had caught her eye, just down from Zhang's perch at an Internet café. This wasn't the expensive sort of place that called to wealthy tourists, but simpler in nature. She smiled and nodded to the young woman who busily arranged sundresses on a rack. The woman gave her a friendly *"Kalimera"* and kept at her work.

Lin wandered through the store, letting her touch be her guide. Color was important to her, but the feel of things often more so. So much of her life centered around touch: the warm feel of Wei, damp from his makeshift bath in her cabin, the pliancy of a client's body after she'd worked the tension away and—soon, she hoped—the feel of being in another man's arms, his body joined with hers.

At the very back of the shop was a rack of nightgowns. Not gowns, actually, but more like the silky little nothings that the ladies' boutique aboard ship sold. Lin flipped through the offerings, and her eyes settled at once on a jade-green bit of fabric. Her fingers told her that it was not real silk, but she liked the texture nonetheless.

She lifted the hanger from the rack and regarded the item with a critical eye. She supposed that with its thin straps and plunging neckline, it might be a slip, meant to be worn beneath a dress, except that it would scarcely cover her bottom, and she was a woman of medium height, at best.

"Very pretty, no?" The saleswoman had come to stand beside her.

"Very pretty."

Lin imagined herself in this and only this, with Gideon's necklace as her sole adornment. Even a woman like her, with limited experience in seduction, knew that she was heading in the correct direction. Lin purchased it without a moment's hesitation.

Small parcel in hand, she wound her way around the streets, returning greetings from those she knew from *Alexandra's Dream*. A few narrow streets over, she found what she sought. It appeared that the Greek letters above the door must indeed mean pharmacy. Lin quickly found more infant formula and even a bottle. She was about to pay when it occurred to her that a woman who planned a seduction must also be practical.

Lin could not count on the fact that she had been a nursing mother until just the other day to impede pregnancy. And she could not forget that as much as her heart was beginning to cry otherwise, her time with Gideon was meant to be limited. For the first time in her life, Mei Lin Wang bought a box of condoms. Seduction was a detailed business, indeed.

As they had planned before parting ways, Zhang and Lin met by the sea horse fountain in the Plateia ton Martiron Evreon, just before eleven. Zhang had arrived there first and was watching the fountain's splash and dance, her pretty face solemn.

"More bad news?" Lin asked.

"Nothing more on Ji Chan and Quio Chan, but something from Beijing. Two more of the group have disappeared. No one is sure, but it's believed they were taken in for questioning. That makes five in the last month," Zhang said.

Lin didn't ask who. She could deal better with the news if she did not put faces with it.

"It seems they're making a concerted effort to tidy up," Zhang commented. "The Beijing organization has been a shambles since Wei Chan's death."

Lin knew that her friend expected no response. She gazed at the square paving stones beneath her feet. It was all too much to think about…too much to consider. *Breath by breath,* she reminded herself. *Get to Paris and then decide what comes next.*

And at least she knew what she wished to happen tonight….

"In your office I suppose you have a listing of the officers' cabins," she said ever so casually to Zhang as they made their way back to the ship and their afternoon duties.

"I suppose I do," Zhang replied just as casually.

"And if I asked, might you stay in my cabin tonight and watch Wei?"

Zhang's broad smile nearly brought a blush to Lin's face.

"Venturing out tonight?" her friend asked.

"Yes," she replied. "And don't ask me any more questions."

"Questions? Why would I have more questions when I can read it all there on your face?"

Lin heaved a sigh of resignation. "So much for being a woman of mystery, eh?"

Zhang laughed. "I'm just pleased you've remembered that you're a flesh-and-blood woman."

Lin would withhold judgment on her feelings about that until the night was through.

GIDEON HAD LEFT THE SHIP long enough for a stop at the synagogue just off the Square of Jewish Martyrs, which he visited each time he was in Rhodes. He doubted that many of the tourists who walked through that square thought of it as more than "that place with the pretty fountain." But to Gideon, it was much more. Lin had said that he did not value his freedom. She couldn't know how wrong that was.

The Jewish community that once had thrived here was long gone. To stand in this place and know that sixteen hundred Jews had been rounded up from here and shipped off to certain death at Auschwitz was to know in one's soul what freedom meant…and the horrible cost at which it was often obtained. All the more reason to mitigate the damage instead of expand it exponentially, as Lin seemed determined to do.

He wished he could treat her as he did the women he'd known before Rachel. If he were the man he'd been back then, he'd have been able to give pleasure, take pleasure and then move on. But he was older now, battle-scarred and wary. His expectations for himself and those he was with had changed.

Lin was to be in his life for only several days more.

If Rachel's death had taught him anything, it was that life was paved with regrets. He could spend the next several days avoiding Mei Lin Wang. Or he could share passion with her and perhaps persuade her that her chosen path wasn't the only one. In the end, that would be one less regret that he carried with him, and one more lesson learned.

Gideon left the place of the martyrs and returned to the land of the living.

That afternoon, off the coast of Elba, Italy

DANTE COLANGELO was being haunted by Napoleon's ghost.

"Able was I ere I saw Elba," he said.

The yacht's crewman standing at the rail with him gave a quizzical tilt of his head. *"Che?"*

Dante shook his head. What was the point in explaining a palindrome that an English language teacher had taught him a million years ago? Odd that he even recalled it….

Napoleon had been exiled by the British to Elba, and Dante's superiors had shipped him off here. To Dante's way of thinking, he had two choices: he could make the best of it, or he could let *la bella strega* down below drive him mad.

She was not as shallow as she wanted him to believe. Neither was he so dense as he chose to have her believe. They each protected their true identities. And if he were a romantic—which he was not—he'd say that they each protected their souls.

Dante glanced at his watch. He'd left Ariana to her own devices long enough. With a nod to the crewman, he returned to the witch's world, down below.

Ariana was pacing the small salon. The food he'd brought her for lunch remained untouched, sitting on the low table by the sofa. He sat down and took a bite out of a piece of the crusty peasant bread that she'd ignored. She had no idea what she was missing.

"You should eat," he told her. "This is very good."

"*Eat?*"

Again, anger tinged her voice, but Dante was not surprised.

"I don't burn enough energy down here to need more food. In fact, I'm beginning to feel like a mushroom, being kept in the dark and fed—"

Dante slammed the flat of his hand on the table, making the dishware jump. "*Basta!* Enough!"

Ariana wheeled away from him and looked longingly toward the cabin door. "What's the harm in letting me go above deck? I really need some air."

"The harm, Ariana, is that I don't trust you."

She held out her arms, and her blue eyes grew icy. "What do you think I'm going to do, signal someone? Care to search me for flares?"

"I know you have no flares. I also know that the less you know, the safer you'll be. If you know nothing, you can say nothing."

"Safe? From who? I've already been kidnapped!"

He shook his head. They would chase each other in circles for yet another day unless he ended it. "No more. Play nice."

"I want to go home, okay?"

Dante hated that he heard tears in her voice. And he knew exactly how she felt. He, too, wanted to go home.

Napoleon had been right. Exile stank.

GIDEON WOKE WITH A START and listened for the sound that had intruded on his sleep.

Had he been dreaming of mice?

How else to explain that scratching sound…like the mice that had nibbled their way into the walls of his grandfather's farmhouse when Gideon was a child.

Again he heard it, and it seemed to be coming from the corridor. Gideon switched on the bedside lamp and slipped from bed. He quietly opened a dresser drawer, then pulled on a pair of boxer shorts. If a trip into the hallway was required, best that he not be nude.

Now semiattired, he looked through his door's spy hole, and could not have been more surprised. Lin waited in the corridor, her arms wrapped around her waist so tightly that he wondered if it might hurt. Stranger yet, she looked to be dressed for rain, in a tan raincoat buttoned to the neck.

"Interesting choice of clothing," he said once he'd ushered her into his cabin.

"Interesting lack of clothing," she replied, but not with the spark he was accustomed to hearing in her voice.

He supposed that a case of nerves might be natural enough, considering she was creeping around the officers' quarters in a raincoat. Gideon watched with great interest as she brought her hands to that coat's tortoiseshell buttons.

"My coat seemed a better choice than walking the hallway in this," she said as she worked the last button. Lin slipped out of the garment in question and then draped it over the back of one of his two club chairs.

Gideon's mouth went dry. He'd had women approach him time and again since he'd come to work on *Alexandra's Dream*. In a purely objective sense, some of them had been more beautiful than Lin. But not one of them had sent his heart slamming the way the simple sight of her did.

"I'm here to seduce you," she announced.

That much Gideon had already figured out. By her nervous expression, Lin had not yet looked at him closely enough to note that this was to be one of the easiest seductions on record. Of course, who was he to deprive a woman of her sense of empowerment?

"Really?" he asked, then walked back to his bed, where he settled in on the pillows, hands crossed behind his head. "Seduce away."

She frowned. "I hadn't considered the steps past getting in this room."

"But a good warrior should always have a battle plan."

"This isn't war."

He grinned. "You think not?"

"What do you mean?"

"What I mean is this—I'll share my body with you, but I will also share my mind. I'm not a machine, Lin, here to give you physical satisfaction and nothing else. If that's what you seek, I believe there are other ways to obtain that. But if you're bold enough—"

"*This* is not bold enough?" she asked with an impatient flick of her hand at her chosen outfit.

"—*and* if you're sure enough of what you want for your future that you can withstand a little persuasion, come closer to this bed," Gideon finished as though she had not interrupted him.

Lin hesitated. She must be giving his words serious consideration. Gideon thought she might put her coat back on and flee. If that was her chosen course, it would take all of his willpower not to race to the door and bar it before she could leave, but he'd meant what he'd said. She wasn't getting the body without the soul.

"Or you can just stand there until morning," he offered as an alternative. "But I'd expect with so little on, you'd catch a chill."

He measured time by the heavy beat of his heart. Her smile was slow in arriving, but once it was there, it was electric.

"Wise choice," he said to her.

She lifted her hands to the back of her head, and Gideon was riveted by the way her breasts moved beneath the sleek green fabric that barely covered them. When she shook her hair free, though, he could think of nothing other than touching it.

"Come over here," he said, pushing the words past the hunger that had tightened even his throat.

She walked to the edge of the bed, grace in every step. "Am I close enough?"

"Almost." His fingers damn near burned with the need to touch her, *now*.

"Better?" she asked, placing both palms on the mattress so that her hair hung loose in front of her.

She was within his reach.

"Anticipation is essential to seduction, don't you think?" he asked, tracing one finger along the neckline of her slip…or whatever one called the bit of fabric she wore.

"Absolutely," she replied, drawing her legs up on the bed until she knelt over him.

As she gazed down at him, he realized what a mystery she remained to him: a fragile warrior. There had been no one since Rachel, no one in his bed and no one who had worked her way into his consciousness as Lin had.

Gideon's breath hitched when she placed her hand over his chest.

"I can feel your heart, here," she said. "But I can also feel it in your words. That makes this easier for me, and I thank you."

She would have to seduce him another time. Gideon had reached the limits of his self-restraint….

HOW QUICKLY ONE'S WORLD could change. One instant Lin was feeling Gideon's fast and solid heartbeat beneath her palm, and the next minute she was beneath him.

"Enough anticipation," he said, and Lin knew a

moment's disappointment. A rush to completion was not her desire. They were destined to have so little time together that she wanted to go slowly, to savor each minute. But then he began scattering kisses along her forehead and sifting his fingers through her hair.

"I have wanted to do this almost from the first moment I saw you," he said.

"Please do, and for as long as you wish." She relaxed into his touch, letting her head sink deeper into the pillow and her face tilt up toward his.

He smiled down at her. "We'll have to settle for as long as I can. I want you too much, Lin."

She drew his face down to hers and began to explore his mouth. She loved the stroke of his tongue against hers, the way they melded into one being, breath and soul and heartbeat.

Lin hadn't realized how much she had been starved for a man's touch. With her husband's death, she had shut down this part of her identity. Focusing only on survival, she had let her mind bury memories of pleasure in a deep, icy cave. But now, she had begun to awaken again, to feel her body come alive after an endless winter.

He broke their kiss long enough to touch the jade pendant. "It's warm," he said. "Almost like a living thing."

She nodded.

He settled the pendant back into place, then kissed the patch of skin just above it. "Beautiful jade…it suits you."

"Thank you."

She placed a hand in the middle of his chest, gently urged him onto his back and settled herself above him.

"May I?" she asked.

"Of course, but you've seen me."

"Not all of you, and not in the same way."

She knew his body well, but in an impersonal sense. Tonight she could explore and delight over what she'd had to block from her mind when he lay on her massage table. She let her fingers glide over what she'd touched so many times before—the rise of muscle at his shoulders, with the hard curve of bone beneath. But now she could linger on his chest, on the slope of pectoral muscles well formed from years of activity, on the dusting of brown hair at the center of his chest, over the flat male nipples so different from her own.

She had never been a seductress, but fancied she knew what one might do. Lin leaned forward and kissed a line down the center of his abdomen, following the thin trail of hair that bisected his body. The rise and fall of his chest told her that he took pleasure from her attention. She stopped at the waistline of his boxer shorts and then dipped one finger below.

"You may keep on as little or as much clothing as makes you comfortable," she said, as though they were back in her massage room.

"Less, I think, would be more comfortable," Gideon replied.

He raised his hips from the bed, and she worked the silken burgundy boxers off him, and then dropped them on the floor at the foot of the bed. Lin paused a moment to look at him. These particular parts of him she had never seen before. He was, as elsewhere, bold and strong and quite perfect in her eyes.

She let her gaze travel upward and saw that he had been watching her. His mouth curved into a smile, but he said nothing. He was, as she'd known from the first time he'd entered her massage room, a man comfortable in his own skin. He certainly had every right to be. She let her hand slowly trail across the flesh that she had exposed and smiled a woman's smile of power when he involuntarily flexed under her touch.

"Do that much more and it will be a very short night," Gideon said.

Because she wanted to be fair, she tugged off her bit of covering and let it slide to the floor, too. Gideon said something low and swift and decidedly not in English. She knew by the look in his eyes, though, that it was good.

"I also meet with your approval, then?" she asked.

"You exceed it." He sat up and eased her back onto the pillows, making sure that she was comfortable. The sheets felt cool against her skin.

"Let me explore you," he said.

She could think of nothing she wanted more.

Gideon was a thorough man. By the time he'd kissed and stroked and touched as he wished, Lin was damp with desire and ready to beg.

"I want to feel you inside me," she said. "Now."

"Damn," he said, sitting up and running one hand

through his hair, which was already tousled from their lovemaking. "I didn't think about…"

She knew what had stopped Gideon. "Ah, but I did."

Lin slipped from the bed and retrieved her morning's purchase of condoms from her coat pocket. "Warriors must have a plan, which means there must be exactly one warrior in this room, after all."

She returned to the bed and handed him the box of condoms. He gave her a deep kiss.

"And you're a wise warrior, too," he said.

Lin stretched out on the bed next to him and watched as he readied himself. The room was quiet, so much so that Lin fancied she could hear the heady rush of her blood through her veins. Done with his preparations, Gideon came to her and settled his weight above her.

It had been so long since she'd experienced this moment, both intimate and exciting. She looked up into his gray eyes, which seemed to Lin to be darker with desire. She ran her hand along the hard line of his jaw, rough with stubble at this late hour of the night.

"You're sure?" he asked.

She could not live the rest of her life without knowing this man. Lin answered without words, tilting her hips up to accept him. He entered her slowly, giving her body a chance to adjust. Lin felt pleasure as he filled her, but also a whisper of sorrow.

Before this moment, she had known only Wei Chan's touch, the feel of Wei within her. But he was gone, and she lived. It was not wrong to live fully, but it also felt as though she was now fully and finally admitting that

Wei Chan was no more. Lin closed her eyes tighter, but the tears still seeped from beneath her lashes. She wished that she had thought to turn off the light before coming back to bed.

Gideon paused.

She had known he was an observant man, though right now she wished he were a little less so.

"Do you want me to stop?" he asked.

Lin could feel him hard and deep within her, and knew what an effort he made to still. She adored him all the more for it.

"No. Just give me a moment...."

He used the pad of one thumb to wipe a tear from her face. "Lin, unless we're both careful, this will be a very crowded bed."

"I'm sorry. I just drifted away for a moment."

"Then come back to me. I'm the man above you...the one inside you. The one who wants you to feel how much I want you."

He began to move deliberately, easing in and out of her while sipping kisses from her mouth and whispering to her how wonderful it felt to make love to her.

Love.

She would not let her mind travel that road. Tonight was about pleasure, about reawakening. Lin wrapped her legs high around Gideon's back, gasping at the new sensations that washed over her.

He kissed her hard, his tongue echoing the joining of their bodies. She felt consumed by him, drawn into a fire she had no wish to escape. Faster he moved, and deeper, too. Heavens, how she loved what he was doing to her.

Love.

This is not love, she reminded herself.

"Lin, look at me."

She did as he asked, though it brought more intimacy to the act than she was quite willing to give.

"The two of us. We share this. Leave the rest," he demanded.

Then he left her no choice at all, pushing her beyond the brink. Lin arched and cried out, shaking with the pleasure she'd missed for so long.

But it was *not* love.

CHAPTER ELEVEN

It SEEMED THAT ONE BREATH at a time might be too much to ask. Though Lin's body was sated, her mind still whirled. She wasn't sure if she should have run from Gideon before making love with him last night, or if she should run back into his arms this morning. All she knew for certain was that her world had changed. Slipping from his bed, well before dawn, to return to her cabin had been difficult. She had loved the feel of his arms around her. Loved it far too much.

Now, when she should have been preparing her massage room for her nine o'clock client, she instead found herself instinctively seeking the peace of the ship's library. The posh space was lovely, with its thick carpet underfoot, display cases of antiquities, comfortable chairs and trove of books.

To Lin, it seemed a bit desolate. She still expected to have Ariana greet her with her broad smile and eyes a rich blue Lin was sure she'd never see again...until she saw Ariana. She would not give up the hope.

There was much she wished she could share with her friend, even tell her of her feelings for Gideon. Not that Lin was too sure what those feelings were.

Desire? Certainly.

Respect? Of course. He was an accomplished man, and smart, too. She knew that luck was the only reason he had not yet caught wind of the fact that baby Wei was aboard.

Today they were in Santorini. Tomorrow, this cruise would end. They would be in Piraeus, the port that served Athens. She could, she supposed, slip away then, instead of waiting for this upcoming, final cruise which she'd committed to work.

But departing now would leave her no time with Gideon. The thought brought a tight chill to her heart. Not yet… Her destiny must include some measure of personal happiness, no matter how brief.

Lin settled into an armchair, closed her eyes and drew a deep breath. She craved calm, and knew that had to start from within. She cleared her mind of the day's worries, and of what her future might hold. If she centered herself, the rest should follow.

"Meditating?"

No need to open her eyes to know who asked the question. She'd heard that same voice low in her ear last night, telling her how beautiful she was. She felt her mouth curve into a full, welcoming smile.

Love?

Infatuation, she told herself. That would be why she already hungered for his touch again.

Lin looked up at Gideon. He seemed younger this morning, and the lines that usually fanned out from the corners of his eyes were softer. His eyes, themselves, weren't as stone-hard as they sometimes seemed, either. He looked…content. Had she done that for him? Did she, too, look different?

"Good morning," she said.

He sat in the chair nestled beside hers, and she wished she could reach out and touch his hand where it rested so close to her own. Now that she had known his touch, she wondered how she would keep up the fiction of being just another face on the ship when their paths crossed. Very poorly, she suspected.

"Good morning," he said. "Did you get any sleep when you returned to your cabin?"

"A little," she lied. Actually, she had given Wei a bottle, then cuddled with him until the sky grew light, and Zhang awoke and grilled her with questions. Questions which Lin had declined to answer…nosy friend!

"You should have awakened me before you left."

She shook her head. "You looked too comfortable. I wanted you to rest."

"And I would have wanted to kiss you goodbye."

A couple entered the room, and Lin gave Gideon a cautionary shake of her head before rising. Much as she loved the library, she would not stay when guests were there. It was their place, not hers.

Gideon rose, too. "I'll walk you to the spa," he said to Lin after saying good morning to the room's new occupants.

"No, thank you," she replied, as though he'd offered her a sweet. She thought quickly of some way to tell him that she would be free that night. "I'll be sure the schedule is cleared for your seven o'clock appointment, sir."

A slight quirk of the right corner of his mouth was the only evidence that he found her approach amusing.

"Seven o'clock, Miss Wang," he said.

"Yes, sir."

Alone in the elevator from Bacchus deck to her place of work, Lin accepted her choice. She would risk another week aboard *Alexandra's Dream*. Really, that was nothing compared to what she feared she'd already offered up: her heart.

GIDEON STOOD IN FRONT of one of the library's display cases, gazing at some piece of bric-a-brac or another. Usually he had an eye for detail, but this morning he had eyes only for Lin. Of course, she had exited the room with her usual quiet grace, leaving him alone except for the elderly couple who wandered the space as if lost. He almost resented their arrival. They'd made Lin feel the need to flee.

Tonight, though, he would steal his time with her. Tonight he would feel whole and alive again. He couldn't and wouldn't define what he felt for Lin. He knew only that he felt a vitality he hadn't experienced since Rachel's death.

Last night, loving Lin had helped him reach one solid realization. He was damn tired of being alone, and the only way to fix that was to make some changes in his life. If he returned to his job with the Mossad, his past would follow him every step of the way. Those he worked with all knew Rachel, all knew what he'd been through. He didn't have the appetite to see the pity in their eyes, or the patience to wait for that pity to fade.

Beyond that, he had changed. Maybe it was a function of growing older, or maybe he'd just grown soft, but he didn't have the desire to live on the edge anymore. He wanted to be able to relax, to have a normal life with friends not in the business, as all of his and Rachel's had been. He wanted to vacation and have it be a *real* vacation. He wanted to have no worry greater than where, when he was old and gray, he would spend his retirement.

And he wanted children. The only reasons he didn't have one or two by now were his job and Rachel's wishes. Rachel was gone from his life, and he was free to leave the Mossad, should he so choose.

Free. Gideon laughed aloud as he considered the concept. He was free! He'd felt bound to his old life and his old duties for so long, but it seemed that he'd been the one enslaving himself. The world awaited him. He could see it from this ship or any other place he chose!

He turned away from the display he'd been blind to and prepared to focus on his future. Instead, he almost bumped into the older man who seemed to have crept up behind him, and was peering into the case Gideon had just turned from.

"Sorry," he said, fighting back a smile. Damn good thing that in his future he'd be dealing with civilians, and not spies and assassins. If a portly man nearing eighty could surprise him, it was definitely time to go.

"Have a wonderful day," he said to the older couple before leaving the library. Based on the bemused looks they gave him, he guessed he must be grinning like a fool, after all.

Gideon briskly returned to his office. There, he found Sean Brady in his chair.

"If you're trying it on for size, you'll have to wait your turn," he said. "Now, up. I've got work to do, and so do you. Why don't you go see what the good Father Connelly has scheduled in the way of tours for the next cruise? Or better yet, go see the good Father Connelly?"

Instead of handing him some good-natured complaining, Brady gave him an odd look.

"What?"

"You're scaring me, boss. Did somebody slip some sunshine in your cereal this morning? You look different." Brady tilted his head in appraisal. "Dare I say *happy?*" He'd spoken the last word as though it could be equated with a virulent disease.

"I'll be happier yet when you get about your business," Gideon said pointedly.

Grinning, Brady gave him a sharp salute and was gone.

Gideon reclaimed his desk, settled his hand over his computer's mouse and pulled up the pending incident reports. The number of reports still lingering made him frown.

It wasn't just in his personal life that he'd lost focus. He hadn't been performing poorly here on *Alexandra's Dream,* by any means. But he hadn't been performing up to his personal standards, either. There would be no more wallowing in self-pity, and no more stopping simply because some corporate procedure indicated that he'd done all that was required of him. His gaze lingered on one name in particular...Ariana Bennett.

Gideon opened up his e-mail files, searching for the address of an old friend—one who'd gone to work at Interpol's Command and Coordination Center about the time Gideon had joined Liberty Line. Alec, a Brit who made James Bond look rough around the edges, owed him a few favors, dating back to the wild days when Arafat had fallen ill and the information flood-gates had slammed shut. Gideon would pull those favors now.

And as long as he was asking questions, he'd satisfy some personal curiosity. China was a member nation of Interpol, and while not exactly free with information, stuff of a basic nature was available. If Alec combed files while Gideon did the same through other sources, surely something could be gleaned about a student activist named Wei Chan, and perhaps even Mei Lin Wang.

Gideon leaned back in his chair as he considered his intentions. Even though he'd made a career of intrusion, it didn't sit well to do so with Lin. But he couldn't continue to go forward as though her future meant nothing to him. Philosophical issues aside, he didn't like the idea of Lin Wang plunging herself into the thick of Chinese politics. It took no special intuition or knowl-edge to see that one slender woman would be eaten up in the machinery of Beijing. It had happened decades ago at Tiananmen Square, and he had no doubt that it could happen again. Lin would share no more details of her past, not after he'd reacted so strongly already. Still, he needed to know more. How else was he to protect her, even if she wasn't quite his to protect?

Once he'd located Alec's e-mail address, Gideon pulled out his keyboard and began composing a message to his old friend.

Two women, each with their own mysteries. Ironic that Gideon had more right to be asking about Ariana Bennett than he did Lin Wang. His hand hovered over the computer mouse for a moment, but in the end, he took the step he needed to.

"Message sent" flashed on Gideon's computer screen.

Now he would wait….

MONEY.

Megaera would never have enough of it. Money was useful, certainly, for the things it bought her. She was a woman who required her luxuries. Sleeping on less than thousand-count Porthault linens was for the masses, not her.

Far more important was the information that money could send flying her way. And information had a wonderful way of leading to the means to acquire more money. In Megaera's experience, crime paid, and handsomely, too. But sometimes one also had to give up some money in the near term, in order to later achieve a greater reward.

As she prepared the instructions for funds to be transferred from her offshore account to one held by her Interpol contact, she frowned at the sum required. Megaera despised greed...unless it was her own.

Megaera despised bad news, too. Her Interpol contact had hardly been a ray of sunshine on the phone this morning. Dire phrases like "suspicions have been aroused" and "the pipeline is drying up" had been bandied about. Fifty thousand euros had best oil that pipeline. If not, there were other ways to deal with poor contacts.

Megaera was no pacifist.

CHAPTER TWELVE

"ONE BREATH IN... One breath out..." Lin instructed Zhang.

Heaven knew she was qualified to give advice on finding one's center. Her final cruise aboard *Alexandra's Dream* had begun. Lin was feeling something like optimism. Zhang, on the other hand, was feeling something like exhaustion. More than any other group aboard ship, housekeeping bore the sting of back-to-back cruises, which left little time to turn the rooms of departing passengers, let alone give the ship the sparkle and polish for which it was renowned.

It was now nearly six, and the ship was due to leave the port of Piraeus. Most assuredly all were aboard who were coming aboard. Zhang lay facedown on the spare bed in Lin's cabin. Lin lay on the other bed next to Wei, who was showing his prodigious strength by pushing himself up on his wobbly arms.

"Soon our little warrior will be walking," Lin said to Zhang.

"Not before next week, I hope," Zhang mumbled into the pale blue bedspread. "I'll never keep up with him." She rolled onto her side and propped up her head with her hand. "Were you able to make your plans to get to Paris?"

"Yes, everything is set."

While Zhang had been supervising her end of this miracle renewal of the ship, Awa had watched Wei, and Lin had ventured into Athens and purchased train tickets for a roundabout trip to Paris. The long voyage would be arduous, but she felt more comfortable about their safety than she would in taking the direct route.

She had also phoned her contacts in Paris to discuss her living arrangements. For the first few months, until she could get back on her feet, she and Wei would be living with a group of students, and she would be doing translation work for a local immigrants' aid office.

Lin was having a difficult time imagining how her apartment-mates would deal with a baby in their midst, but she and Wei had already survived stranger situations. She picked up her son and planted a kiss on his baby-smooth cheek.

"Not much longer, my love," she said to him.

Their secret knock sounded at the door.

"That will be Awa," Zhang said. "No doubt she's done her spying and is ready to tell us of all the handsome men who have come aboard."

Lin laughed. Poor, tired Zhang couldn't have sounded less interested.

"Well?" Lin asked once Awa had hurried in, her lovely face aglow with excitement.

"So far, we have confirmed two American baseball

players, and then someone that Maya from housekeeping thinks might be a pop star."

"Any reason why?" Zhang asked.

"Bodyguards," Awa replied.

"Ah."

Alexandra's Dream had already seen its share of notables, so it took more than a couple of sports figures or a potential pop star to rouse much interest.

"We even saw a man with your eyes," Awa said. "Though he was much too old for me to waste my time looking at very long."

"My eyes?" Zhang asked. "You mean eyes too dry and sleepless to stay open another moment?"

The teenager shook her head. "No, I mean shaped like yours...not all round like mine."

"Chinese, then," Zhang said.

Awa shrugged. "Or Japanese or something. As I said, he was too old for me to care. And you all look the same to me," she added with a cheeky grin.

Zhang snorted, and Lin had to laugh, too.

But, then, the more that she thought about what Awa had said about this man, the more her stomach rolled in a most uncomfortable way.

"You don't think..." she began saying to Zhang.

Zhang waved her off with one lazy hand. "Later. We'll worry about one guest among a thousand later. Right now, I need to rest."

But right now, Lin needed to put her mind at ease.

"Would you stay with Wei for just a little while?" she asked Awa. "I'd like to stretch my legs, if I could."

Awa nodded. "And I would like to rest mine."

Ten minutes later, Lin hovered behind the crowd at the ship's rail, cheering as *Alexandra's Dream* disembarked. She knew that she was being silly, thinking that she might spot one man with almond eyes in this gathering, if Awa had really even seen him in the first place. Still, she had to try.

Satisfied that no such man was on deck, she moved back inside and began what she realized was likely a futile tour of the four passenger decks with public rooms. Even if futile, it made her feel better because she was doing *something*.

She made a quick circuit of the Helios deck's indoor space and spotted no one threatening, unless she counted Dima Ivanov glowering at her when she took a peek in the fitness center. Lin hopped back into the elevator and pushed the button for the next deck down.

The Court of Dreams was the aptly named and gloriously ornate main lounge on the Artemis deck. The scent of roses from flower arrangements adorning the lounge's tables wafted through the air. A pianist was seated at the shiny black grand piano in the center of the room, playing a beautiful classical melody. Lin tried to be unobtrusive as she scanned the couples sitting on the plump brocade sofas and chairs.

At the far end of the large room, she saw Gideon. Last night they had managed to find an hour or so to spend together, but with the change in cruise passengers, he'd told her that he'd be quite occupied today.

It was almost as if he sensed her presence because

he glanced away from the guests he was chatting with, and his gaze met hers. She felt a delightful warmth come over her…the warmth of knowing that she, Mei Lin Wang, was admired and desired. She smiled, trying to put into that simple act how much she, too, admired and desired him.

Then a shiver coursed down her spine, almost as though someone had turned up the ship's air-conditioning full blast. Someone—or something—was watching her in this place of dreams. Seeking the presence, Lin looked away from Gideon and to her left—toward the sweeping divided staircase. Instead of a man with almond eyes, she saw two women in garishly bright cruise wear loudly giggling about Scarlett O'Hara as they descended the marble stairs. Neither had noticed Lin at all. What, then, had she felt?

Lin tried to shake off the ill feeling, telling herself that she was being morbidly fanciful. She glanced back at Gideon. Concern was clear on his handsome features. When he looked as though he might head her way, she gave a small shake of her head. Even if she desired his comfort, she could not have it. She could no more tell him of baby Wei's grandparents than she could of Wei. And so she would deal with this on her own.

Lin left the Court of Dreams, but all the way back to her cabin, she could not lose the feeling that a ghost had settled on her shoulder. Had Wei Chan come to visit and warn her of approaching dangers?

GIDEON WALKED ONE CIRCUIT of the crowded tavernlike room where the crew did its socializing. The dimly lit barroom was awash in languages, men and beer. He'd been mad—and desperate—to think that he might find Lin in this crowd. He was madder yet for what he was about to do.

He needed to see her, to find out why she had suddenly looked so pale and frightened in the Court of Dreams. And if he were going to be honest with himself, if he hadn't witnessed that moment, he'd still need to see her, anyway. He wouldn't hash through the whys or hows of her growing presence in his thoughts. He would just deal with it.

Gideon took the crew elevator down to the lower deck where Lin's cabin was located. The corridor was not empty, but those who saw him knew better than to do more than nod a polite greeting. The two and a half stripes he wore on his uniformed shoulders carried certain advantages.

He reached Lin's door and knocked on it. Someone stirred inside, and a moment later, the door opened a crack.

Lin peeked out. Her hair was down about her shoulders. Gideon had to stop himself from reaching out and sifting his fingers through it.

"May I come in?" he asked instead.

Lin hesitated.

"Are you busy?"

"Not busy," she said in a low voice. "I have let my friend Zhang sleep in here. Her roommate snores horribly, and she's very tired after today. Zhang is in charge of the laundry, you see."

"Ah. Then will you come to my cabin?"

Again, she hesitated.

"Please. I need to see you."

She seemed to let go of whatever was holding her back. "And I need to see you, too. Go…and I will be with you as soon as I can."

GIDEON DID NOT WAIT patiently in his cabin. Lin had become a fire under his skin that tonight would not quench. He knew that making love to her again would make it burn all the brighter, but he wanted her just the same. Just when he was ready to go find her and bring her to him, a soft knock sounded at the door.

Gideon opened it, wrapped his hand about her slender wrist and quickly hauled her inside. Her hair swung around her like a flag of dark silk, tempting him even more.

"I don't—" she began to say.

He shook his head. "No talk now. Just touching." He busied himself with the row of white buttons that marched down the front of her pale yellow blouse. "Later, we'll talk."

She must have seen the merit to his plan, for her hands grew just as busy with his clothing.

Never with Rachel had he felt this desperation…this primal need to own and to be owned. He had Lin naked and sprawled on his bed in a matter of moments. She held out her arms to him, inviting him to take her.

She wouldn't have to ask twice. Gideon let his mouth

travel her body, tasting her, imprinting her on his mind. If he was not to have her long, he would have her well.

She was ready for him, and he was beyond ready. He reached for the condom he'd stashed beneath the pillow before she'd arrived, opened the packet with a shaking hand and rolled the condom into place. As he did, a mad thought came into his mind…. How would it feel to make a child with this woman? To know that as they loved, a new life might be created?

Madness, indeed.

Gideon surged into her and drew a sharp breath at the wash of sensations that came over him. Hunger, need, relentless urge, but also a sense of rightness…a sense of belonging.

He looked down at her. She wore much the same shocked expression he expected was on his face. He knew he hadn't hurt her. Her hum of pleasure when he'd entered her had told him that. What then?

"This is how it's supposed to be, isn't it?" he asked.

Simple words, but with not such a simple effect.

"It is," she said, smoothing her hands down his sides, as though to comfort him.

He closed his eyes against the tenderness in her expression. Passion was one thing. This offer of something more from a woman who'd already announced her intention to march from his life and into certain disaster was more than he could handle.

Gideon pushed them both harder, faster…beyond tenderness to pure response. Every muscle in his body tightened as the need for release consumed him. But not yet… Not until she understood what she was giving up…

"You'd walk from this?" he asked, his voice breathless and rasping. "You'd leave this?"

She held tight to his shoulders, her body arched upward in need.

"Please," she gasped. "Please…*now*."

Gideon gave her what she wanted, even though he knew she'd never do the same in return. And a while later, as she lay there in his arms, passion spent, he could already feel her slipping away.

"Tonight, when I saw you in the Court of Dreams, why did you suddenly look so frightened?" he asked.

"Frightened?" she repeated.

"Yes."

"I didn't look frightened, or if I did, I didn't mean to." She hesitated. "Maybe it was just the press of the crowd."

She was lying. Even if he hadn't been trained to pick up on the subtler cues, the quaver in her voice would have given her away.

"If there was something bothering you, you'd tell me, wouldn't you?" he asked.

"Of course."

Another lie.

She rolled onto her stomach and propped herself up on her arms, resting her leg against his. He played with the ends of her long hair where it brushed against his skin.

"So, tell me about the passengers for this cruise," she

said. "Did you meet anyone interesting tonight? My friend Awa says we have some athletes and maybe a pop star."

Gideon noted the nervousness pinching her mouth and shadowing her eyes. There was no actress about her; she would make a very poor spy. The same lack of guile would also seal her fate as an activist in her homeland. Just the thought of her suffering made him ill. That she'd sign herself up for it made him angry, too.

"It's the usual assortment…nothing out of the ordinary," he replied, his voice harsher than he'd intended. He was turning into a poor spy himself.

She edged her leg away so that they no longer touched. "Oh."

"Are you perhaps looking for a pop star to fall in love with?" he asked, trying to lighten the moment. If he could keep her talking, he might find out what was worrying her…as if everything he already knew shouldn't be enough.

"I'm not looking to fall in love with anyone."

Funny, neither was he, but it seemed to be happening in any case. Ignoring her slight resistance, he drew her closer.

"You understand that you're safe with me?"

"Safe? Of course I am safe."

She seemed determined to dance across the surface of this conversation. All Gideon could hope was that the deeper message was also being accepted.

"It's part of me…of who I am, Lin. I protect what's mine." Or at least he tried to. He had failed miserably with Rachel, and he'd be damned if he would again. "I have the feeling that more is going on with you than what you have shared. I can't help you…can't protect you…unless you let me in." He'd tried to tell her that with his body, but seemed to have gotten nowhere.

Lin rolled to a seated position. "You forget one thing. It's not your duty to protect me. I cannot be yours." She left the bed and began to gather her clothes. "I must leave, but may I use your shower first?"

Gideon nodded his consent.

And long after Lin had showered, dressed and departed, Gideon stared at the ceiling and considered her choice of words. She *could not* be his…as though the matter were entirely out of her hands. Finding hope in something so bleak was out of Gideon's character, but then again, so was falling incautiously and totally in love. Which was just what Gideon Dayan had done.

IF THERE WAS NO REST for the wicked, there was even less respite for the worried. After leaving Gideon's cabin, Lin had roused Zhang and badgered her until she'd agreed to go to her office and help Lin…so long as Lin promised to never again, in her natural life, awaken her. It had seemed a decent bargain to Lin.

Zhang finished scanning the room list that she had access to for laundry deliveries.

"No Chans?" Lin asked, her heart still drumming a scarily rapid beat.

The only time she'd been able to let go of the thought that she was being haunted was when she'd been in

Gideon's arms…and then with his concern, he'd resurrected that ghost.

"Not that I see," Zhang said.

Lin nudged her friend away from the computer. "Let me look."

Zhang sighed, but moved away nonetheless.

Lin planted herself in front of the bluish glow of the monitor. Five hundred cabins…nearly a thousand guests on a cruise as booked as this… It was a great deal of information through which to sort.

"Wei and I will just take a nap here in the corner while you have a look," Zhang said.

Wei, wonderful baby that he was, had barely stirred when Lin had put the protective covering over his basket and readied him for some late-night travels. Now he sucked on his pacifier and entertained himself by kicking his legs like a budding football star.

Slowly, carefully, Lin reviewed the list. There was a slight scattering of Japanese surnames, but nothing remotely Chinese. Lin heaved a sigh of relief.

"I have been worrying myself over nothing, when one would think that I have enough that's real to worry about."

She stood and picked up Wei's basket. "Shall we go back to bed?"

Zhang didn't move from her cross-legged position on the floor. "I've just remembered something…. You know that passengers don't have to use their real name on this list. When they book the cruise and board, they do, but after that…"

That horrible rolling feeling gripped Lin's stomach once again. "So Wei's parents could be on board?"

Zhang nodded. "Maybe. Movie stars and the like always use another name, so what's to stop anyone else? According to lists I've had before, Mary Poppins and Rip Van Winkle have been aboard, along with seven John Smiths, all at the same time."

"You're supposed to say something to reassure me!"

Zhang stood. "Reassurance... Hmm... How's this? Do not forget that I know what Wei's parents look like, even if you do not. It has been several years, but they cannot have changed that much.

"Tomorrow, I'll look about the passenger decks after my morning meeting with the director of housekeeping. And we can also ask Awa and Cambro to have their trusted friends on the housekeeping staff keep an eye out. Is that reassurance enough?"

Not really, but Lin knew it would have to be.

CHAPTER THIRTEEN

"YOU ARE LATE," Helga the dragon announced as Lin rushed past her desk.

"I know I am!"

"Wait!"

Lin spun back to face the receptionist.

"I took the liberty of saving your skinny bottom and rescheduled your nine o'clock appointment for seven-thirty, tonight," Helga said. "You will not mind working later when it is your own fault, will you?"

How well the dragon delivered a lecture from behind those sharp teeth....

"Thank you," Lin said, though it galled her to have to do so. Still, Helga had been correct. She *had* over-slept, unwilling to rouse once sleep had finally claimed her. For a brief time this morning, she had even considered calling in sick for the entire cruise. Impossible, but tempting...

Lin took two steps away from the desk, but then Helga reeled her back with another command to wait. Lin knew the receptionist enjoyed this game. Normally, she was willing to play along, too, but not today. She edged away.

"So you don't want to hear about your visitor?"

Lin halted and turned back, her steps less rushed now. "Visitor?"

"Mrs. Saperstein was here. She stayed aboard ship for this leg of the cruise, too. She wants appointments each day."

Lin's patience had fully waned. "Find her time, then."

"Oh, and you had a woman here... Chinese, I think... Or maybe Japanese," she added with a shrug.

Cold beads of sweat popped out on Lin's hands. *One breath at a time,* she reminded herself. One panicked breath at this point, but she needn't share her fear.

"And did this woman want an appointment?"

"No, just a list of services."

"Did she ask for me by name?"

Helga snorted. "You think that you are that famous? Of course she didn't. She did ask if we had anyone Chinese on staff. I told her about you."

"And did you not find that strange?"

"It's not mine to find strange. Why all the questions?"

"To get the answers I require," Lin replied, fighting down her panic. "You must remember something about her."

Helga shrugged. "She was older than you, but younger than me."

Lin gave up the chase and retreated to her massage room. She checked the appointment sheet that Helga had left on the table for her. No Chans, no John Smiths and no Mickey Mouse, either. Before preparing for her next client, Lin eyed her hated telephone and made a tactical decision. She unplugged the little beast. This warrior had faced just about all that she could for one morning.

BY EIGHT-THIRTY THAT EVENING, Lin dragged with a bone-deep and inescapable weariness. Still, she knew she must finish straightening, out her massage room. Other than three hurried visits to Wei, who waited in her cabin with Cambro, she had been captive to her schedule.

Lin was beyond hungry. Her stomach had stopped growling hours ago and fallen into a miserable silence. Before she returned to her son, a stop in the crew's dining room was a necessity.

She gave one last, satisfied look at the order she'd restored in her room. Tomorrow would be smoother than today. Tomorrow she would know her worries about a man with almond eyes and strangers asking about Chinese staff to be as light and passing as the jasmine petals floating in the spa's pool.

Smiling at the thought, Lin swung open the door to her massage room. Some of her newfound calm drifted off; Dima Ivanov waited for her in the hallway.

"Hello, Dima," she said, thinking the best that she could do was put aside their last, ugly encounter and hope that he would do the same.

He returned her smile with something closer to a sneer. Then he pushed himself off the wall he'd been leaning against and held out his hand.

"I have brought you a note from some new friends I made outside the spa today," he said.

Lin hesitated.

"Take it. I think you will find it interesting."

Knowing she had no real choice, Lin reached for the slip of paper and then unfolded it.

Dear heaven.

The note was in Chinese. Lin's mouth went dry and spots danced in front of her eyes. She would not faint. She would not show weakness now, when strength was most needed. Lin stood straighter. She pocketed the slip of paper, hoping that Dima would not see her shaking hand.

"Interesting people who gave me that," he said. "They were also interested when I told them that I am a very great friend of yours...."

"I think we need to find you a word other than *interesting*," Lin said, bluffing a calm she did not feel.

Dima shrugged. "I use what words I know, and in this case, *interesting* suits." He tipped his head and gave her an assessing look. "I did not know you are married, Lin."

Panic took hold of her, body and soul. "I—I *was* married. I am a widow now."

He shrugged, obviously indifferent at best to any pain his questions might be bringing her.

"They asked if you have a baby aboard." His smile was flat, built more of malice than anything else. "You could not be keeping a baby below deck, could you, Lin?"

"Of course not!"

Hands in the pockets of his track pants, he rocked from toe to heel on sneaker-clad feet. "It would be very *int*eresting if you were. Many would like to know of it."

"I don't have a baby," she cried. "How could I possibly, and still work these hours?"

"I don't know…. You have a very powerful friend in Dayan. I would say that if you pay him the right price, you could get away with most anything on this ship."

"Not so long ago you were accusing him of paying me! But you know nothing, Dima…nothing! Now, please, if you are through taking your pleasure at my expense, leave me alone!"

He tipped her face up, his fingers pressing into her until she gasped with pain.

"Pleasure… I had not thought of that. I'll let you know when I'm done with you, Lin. For now, I shall go think on that pleasure."

Dima left, and Lin retreated to her room. She sat down hard on the little chair that had held her and Wei so well. She wanted to cry, but knew if she started, she would never stop.

Reading the note from her in-laws was little more than a formality on one level. They knew about her. They knew about Wei. All else would be disclosed when they were ready.

She reached into her pocket and pulled out the slip of paper, with its Liberty Line insignia at the top. Liberty… A lovely word that she feared was about to become a fiction in her life. A quick reading of the note proved her fear true. Ji and Quio Chan wished to meet her at ten-thirty tonight, here in her massage room. The topic was to be the future of their grandson. If she was not present, as humbly requested, they would immediately report her to the ship's captain.

Stomach roiling, Lin dashed to the bathroom, where she was thoroughly sick, even with nothing in her. After she'd washed her face and hands, she looked at her pallid reflection in the bathroom mirror. She was at sea and could not run from this danger. And even if they were in port, she *would not* run. The time for running had passed.

Was she warrior enough to handle all that she faced?

She had her doubts. Of course, she also didn't doubt that warriors had weak stomachs going into battle. They were only human, too. Even Gideon, for his great strength, was vulnerable.

Gideon...

She could go to him now and tell him all. His shoulders were broader than hers and better suited to this sort of mess—both literally and officially. But if she did so, she would be risking his future, as well.

She knew him and cared for him deeply. Gideon was a protector, which meant that he would no doubt sacrifice himself in order to rescue her. And that, she could not permit. She would have to fight this battle alone.

Lin braced her hands against the cool porcelain of the bathroom sink. *One breath at a time...*until she could breathe no more.

HIS OFFICIAL DAY finally over, Gideon turned to his e-mail. He had yet to hear back from Alec, which did not concern him. He knew he was low on the Briton's priority list, but the passing days also sharpened his impatience. Lin was worrying him, and any small thing he might find to put her behavior into a real-world context would be helpful.

Plenty of mail had arrived today...greetings from his family back in Israel, a quick note from Sean Brady about Father Connelly seeming a little too friendly with a knockout of a new female passenger, and finally...something from Alec!

Gideon began to read...

You're always with the popular crowd, aren't you, friend? It seems that one Ms. Ariana Bennett is of interest to those other than you. Unfortunately, any info on her current status is locked up tighter than a virgin's knees. We shall all go a-begging on that one. So, too, with Mei Lin Wang. I assume you're already aware that she works on your ship? That was all I could find. It is almost as if she has disappeared in her homeland's records. Curious, no? Knowing you, I shall also assume that she is nothing short of gob-smackingly gorgeous. Ergo, your interest.

As for Wei Chan, I had more luck there, though one must wonder why you're interested in a dead, though apparently quite noble, radical. For what it's worth, Mr. Chan fell very far from the family tree.

It seems that his parents are quite high and mighty in the northern town of Jiangsu. The town itself is an industrial wasteland, and the Chans are in charge of industrial licensing. One can only assume that they are as rich as the town is gutted. I've gotten a whisper back that they might have even once been involved

in something dirtier than that, but I'll not talk out of
school, as they say. Will write more when I know.
Take care of yourself, my friend. I think of you often.
Yours,
Alec

"Semi-enlightening," Gideon murmured after saving
Alec's letter to his private mail. There was nothing unsettling on the surface about what he'd read, but there
was also just enough to make him want to dig deeper.
And he would start with a visit to Lin.

Gideon picked up the phone and first called her
room. Another woman answered, one Gideon assumed
was her friend, Zhang. As far as Zhang knew, Lin was
still at work. That didn't surprise him.

Gideon headed directly to the Helios deck. Dima
Ivanov was waiting at the elevator when Gideon exited
it. Ivanov gave him a look that Gideon could best interpret as a smirk, but he didn't bother to engage. His first
interest was in seeing Lin.

He found her heading toward the elevators, once
he'd done his loop of the spa rooms.

"Lin!" he called, hurrying his steps to catch up with her.

She didn't glance back. In fact it looked to Gideon
as though she put her head down in an effort to speed
her pace.

She had hit the bank of elevators' down button by the
time he reached her.

"I've missed you all day. Do you have time to talk?"

"Not now," Lin said.

He looked more closely at her. Instead of a pure, golden ivory, her skin held a grayish cast. Her eyes, too, weren't as clear as usual. It was as though somebody had taken Mei Lin Wang and erased all of her vibrancy.

"Are you ill?" he asked.

She nodded her head. "Yes… It was lunch, I think. Something has not agreed with me."

The elevator in front of them arrived, and Lin quickly hopped inside. When Gideon saw her hand shoot out toward what was no doubt the close button, he gapped the breach and leaped inside, too.

"I'll see you back to your cabin," he said, pressing the appropriate button.

"No. I can—"

"Do *not* tell me that you can do it by yourself," he interrupted.

They finished their ride in a somewhat uncompanionable silence. He escorted her to her door, feeling more like a prison guard than a lover, the way she kept a half step ahead of him at all times.

"Thank you, then," she said when she reached the door. She opened it a bit. Gideon heard a snatch of conversation before she hurriedly closed it again. He was relieved that she'd have someone there to care for her, but would be more relieved if he knew in whose care he'd be entrusting her.

"I'll just pop in and make sure you're settled," he offered.

"No! That would not be proper."

"It's been proper enough when you've come into my room."

"*This* is a woman's room."

Gideon struggled to grasp the distinction, but could find none. Perhaps this was a cultural matter. In any case, he wouldn't quibble. Lin was looking too pale to possibly stand much longer.

"All right. I won't argue with you. But I also want you to call me later. I want to hear your voice and be sure you're taking care of yourself."

"I will do that," she said.

He wanted to take her into his arms, but eyes enough were on them in the narrow corridor.

"Call me, Lin. Promise."

She nodded, and Gideon knew that was as good as he'd be getting. Still, he wanted to give so much more....

LIN HAD NEVER FELT fear like this in her life, not even the day that Wei Chan had been picked up by the authorities. As she walked down the hallway toward her massage room at ten-thirty, she understood how the condemned felt in their last steps. One could hope for a last-minute reprieve, but in one's heart, one knew it wasn't coming.

The couple who waited outside Lin's room looked nothing like Wei Chan had. These people were plump, polished and solemn. Wei Chan had given little thought to his appearance, permitting Lin to cut his hair with her sewing scissors when she could no longer see his eyes.

His clothing had been well mended, but far from new. And he had come from this glossy couple?

She pushed back a shiver of nerves as she approached her in-laws. She greeted them formally, offering them the deference she knew they expected.

"There is little space in my massage room. Perhaps I could show you to some place more comfortable?"

Her father-in-law, a forbidding man for all the fleshiness about his face, shook his head. "No. We will meet here, as I have directed."

Lin said nothing more, and simply opened the door to her small room. The massage table occupied the bulk of the space, with the sole chair taking up what little was left. She gestured at the chair and asked her mother-in-law if she would like to sit, but received no response.

With these two strangers crowding into her own space, Lin chose to stand, too.

"So, you are the girl my son married," Ji Chan said in a way that made it clear he saw no merit in his son's choice.

"I am. We loved each other," she added, even though she had no idea if they'd care.

Ji Chan remained impassive, but it seemed to Lin that a whisper of something passed across his wife's face. Then again, she did not know her at all, and so couldn't be sure.

"You have a son," the father said.

It had been a statement; Lin made no effort to deny it.

"He is well?" Quio Chan asked.

"Quite well," Lin affirmed.

Ji Chan moved a step closer to Lin. "His name?"

It was absurd not wanting to confirm something they likely knew already, but Lin held silent. Too much had been taken from her already.

"There is no reason not to cooperate with us," he said. "We have only our grandson's best interests at heart."

"As you did your son's?" Lin blurted, then immediately wished she could pull back the dangerous words.

"Exactly," Wei's father replied. "Though our son was too headstrong to see it that way."

"We wish to raise our grandson," her mother-in-law said. "We have lost our son to an early death, and now his son should step forward to take what was meant to be Wei's."

Shock freed Lin's tongue. "You're asking for my son? *No!* You must be mad to think that I would even consider it."

Ji Chan raised his hand as though he meant to strike her, but Lin did not back away.

"Mad!" he echoed. "You dare to call us names?"

"You think you could steal my son from me? You *are* mad."

"We are not saying we would take him alone, Mei Lin," her mother-in-law interjected. "You may, of course, live with us, too. We would expect a proper amount of respect from you...not what we've seen here tonight. And you would give us final authority over any matters pertaining to the raising of young Wei."

"I've heard enough," Lin said, trying to push past her

father-in-law. He was too quick, though, and blocked her way to the door.

"You are aware you have a criminal record at home, are you not?" he asked. "You are aware that the Beijing authorities are quite interested in persuading you in for questioning?"

Lin had seen their forms of persuasion, but she would not be cowed by fear in front of this couple. She stood silent.

"We have obtained your records," her father-in-law said. "It is within my power to be sure that they disappear forever. You will be able to return to your home, see your family, do all the things you could do now only at risk of death."

Among her greatest heartbreaks was that her parents did not and could not know where she was. She would trade much in order to be able to safely contact them again.

Much…but *not* her son.

"Did your parents raise a selfish child as well as a willful one, Mei Lin Wang?" her mother-in-law asked in a sharp tone. "We can give our grandson advantages that you could never hope to provide. He will never want for money, and he will be among his own people. What can you offer him? A life of poverty and of being treated as a foreigner wherever he goes. Is that what you wish for him?"

"I wish *love* for him. He is the child of my heart, the reason I could go on after your son was gone. You can never and will never love him as I do!"

Quio Chan's voice grew shrill. "How do you know of our love? How do you know of my suffering when we sent Wei off? Do you think that was done out of cruelty? It was done to save a headstrong boy from ending up dead."

Bitterness filled Lin's heart. "Then your plan didn't work very well, did it?"

Her mother-in-law's face paled, and she fell silent.

"I make my decisions as much for your late son as I do for myself," Lin said. "I am his only voice now that he is gone. And what Wei Chan would say is this—his son is better off living the life of an immigrant than profiting from the ills that Wei Chan fought to expose. We will not be going back home with you."

"You are blinded by emotion," her father-in-law said. "Go and think this night on what we have offered. You would be a fool to turn us down, Mei Lin. And the world does not suffer fools well."

"Better a dead fool than a live traitor to one's own people," Lin said. "You ask the impossible, and I cannot deliver it."

"Tomorrow," her father-in-law said. "Tomorrow, we finish this discussion. First we will see what the night brings."

That, Lin already knew. It would bring more sorrow.

CHAPTER FOURTEEN

GIDEON WAS DREAMING AGAIN, but not of mice. In his sleep he saw Lin, arms tied behind her back and a white cloth over her face, ready to die before a firing squad. And because this was a dream—and only a dream, thank God—Rachel blocked his way when he tried to rescue her.

"This is your destiny," Rachel said. Not Lin's destiny, but his: to lose those that he loved.

Gideon bolted awake. The bedcovers were tangled around his legs, and not to put too fine a point on it, he was in a sweat. As long as he was awake, though, he might as well get on with his day. They'd be making port in Dubrovnik this morning, and he wanted to be sure that Sean Brady stuck close to Father Connelly, who was giving a church tour.

Gideon had just turned on the light and climbed out of bed with the intention of taking a shower when he heard a quiet rapping at his door. Just like the last time, when he peeked through he saw Lin. She was already dressed for work. Unlike last time, he didn't bother to clothe himself.

"It's early to be about," he said to her once he'd let her in.

"I couldn't sleep."

That, he could see. If anything she looked more worn than she had yesterday. Between that and the fact that she'd made no comment about his state of undress, he knew that this was not a morning to tease her, however gently.

"I was about to take a shower," he said. "Maybe you'd like to stretch out on my bed and relax?"

She nodded. Gideon watched as she toed out of her sensible work shoes, then crawled into bed. She hugged his pillow to her chest and inhaled deeply.

He smiled. "What are you doing?"

"Finding comfort."

He was glad that he could give her that, at least. He gestured toward the bathroom. "Stay comfortable, then. I'll be out in a few minutes."

She didn't smile, but some of the tension eased from her features.

"I'll be here," she said.

Gideon wasn't sure how long he stood under the shower, with the warm water pelting away the remnants of the sheer horror that had gripped him as he'd dreamed. In time, though, his muscles relaxed. He tipped back his head and let his mind empty until he was ready to start the day with no lingering stress. It had been a dream...nothing more.

Mind still not quite in the present, Gideon reached for the soap. As he did, to his right, the shower curtain moved. Acting on years of training layered over instinct, he grabbed hard at the arm holding the curtain.

"Gideon, it's me," Lin cried out.

Heart pounding, he released her, then opened the curtain enough to see her in full.

She was nude, except for the necklace he'd given her.

He rather liked her that way.

"You're lucky I didn't kill you," he said as he drew her into his arms and closed the curtain behind them.

"It might have been more merciful," she replied.

At first he thought she'd said that because the spray of water was hitting her directly in the face, so he adjusted their positions.

"Better?" he asked.

She nodded yes, but that meant little when followed by a sob.

"Lin?"

"Just hold me, please," she said.

That, he could do. Anything more and he'd be in un-familiar territory. Gideon was a man, and no better than most when faced with a crying woman. Rachel had seldom cried. She'd been more the sort to literally run her problems into the ground, tying on her shoes and taking off for the university's track.

"Would you like to talk about it?" he asked Lin, and then winced, thinking he sounded like the counselors he'd been compelled to see after Rachel's death.

"No," Lin said. "I just want to feel less alone."

"You're not alone," he said, his formerly hollow heart aching at the pain in her voice. "I promise I'm here for you."

She clung tighter to him and cried in earnest.

And as he held her, feeling as helpless as a man could, Gideon accepted his fate: he wanted to *always* be there for Lin.

FROM LIN'S VANTAGE POINT atop the city wall, the orange tile roofs in Dubrovnik's Old Town glistened like jewels under the late-afternoon sun. It was ironic, her love of cities encased by walls, considering her personal need for freedom. She wished that she had time to actually walk the wall's stone pathway and fully take in the beauty before her, but she'd been blessed to have even a few hours off the ship.

Once she'd finished with her last scheduled appointment, she had decreed to Helga that she would take no walk-ins. Before the dragon could object, Lin had quickly changed from her work uniform to her current garb of a light sundress, in deference to the heat. Still, she could see why few braved the city wall after it had baked under the Croatian sun all day. But Lin relished the quiet moment.

Last night had been the worst of her life, bar none. After leaving her in-laws, she had been terrified for Wei's safety. She did not think it beyond Ji Chan, in particular, to steal her son away. When she'd told Zhang what had happened, they had both agreed that it would be best if Zhang took Wei to a safer spot than Lin's cabin. They had also agreed that until matters settled with her in-laws, Lin should not be near Wei at all.

Zhang knew of one unoccupied stateroom, currently under repair. She'd taken Wei there. And so, for the first night since Wei's birth, Lin had been totally without him. She never wanted to feel that empty again.

Lin tipped her face up to the bold sun, willing it to bring her strength, too. Being held by Gideon this morning had hurt as much as it had brought her comfort. She'd wanted to unburden herself to him, but couldn't, so she'd taken the solace of his arms around her and wished for more.

Soon due back at the ship, Lin made her way down the Pile Gate's steep flight of worn stone stairs and readied herself for the crowds below. She'd gone no more than a dozen steps from the gate when her in-laws fell in step beside her. Fear and anger battled inside her; anger won.

"Did you follow me?" she asked Ji Chan.

"You failed to contact us," he replied, and she took his words for the admission they were.

She sped her pace. "There is nothing more to be said."

Puffing a bit from keeping up with her, Wei Chan's mother took hold of her arm. "Where is our grandson?"

Realizing there was no way to outrun them when they would soon all be on the ship, Lin stopped and moved out of the crowd flowing down the busy walk. Her in-laws followed.

There, under the slight shelter of a coffeehouse's awning, she replied, "*My* son is well tended."

"And we should believe this from you?" Quio Chan asked.

"You have no reason not to. You know me little, and I would prefer that we keep it that way."

"Your preferences, Mei Lin, are not our concern," her father-in-law said.

Lin ignored him. As with Dima Ivanov, he could possess only as much power as she gave him.

"Pretty," her mother-in-law commented.

"What?" Lin asked.

Quio Chan's hand shot out and seized the pendant that Gideon had given Lin.

"This," she said. "Did my son give you this?"

Lin instinctively recoiled, then cried out as the necklace's chain snapped. She caught the thin gold links as they slipped toward the ground.

Quio Chan held the pendant in her hand, her expression as shocked as Lin's.

"Give it back," Lin said. "It's no more yours than my son is."

Her mother-in-law let the jade fall to the walk.

Lin bent and picked it up. It seemed to be in one piece, which was more than she could say for her shattered composure.

"If you two are done…" her father-in-law said.

Lin was beyond done. "No more! I have given you my answer already. Please leave me alone."

"So the day has not brought logic?" Ji Chan asked. "Then consider this…. It is not just your personal records with the authorities that I have seen. I also know that you lied in order to obtain a passport for my grandson. His father is certainly not 'unknown.' One call and I will have the authority to see your passports revoked, Mei Lin. One call."

Lin gripped tighter the jade in her hand. Her lie had been a measured risk. To have listed Wei Chan as father would have guaranteed that she'd never leave China's lands.

"You see what will happen, don't you?" her father-in-law asked. "Without a passport, no other nation will accept you. You and my grandson will be back in your homeland, where his welcome will be much warmer than yours. You are considered a subversive, Mei Lin. Do you think you'll go long without being jailed?"

Lin had never thought herself capable of killing another person, but if she'd had a sword, she would have run them both through.

"You will find life much less comfortable in prison than what we offer you, Mei Lin," Ji Chan said. "Think carefully. We will give you until the ship arrives in Corfu, the day after tomorrow. If you have not come to see what is best for our grandson, we will first visit with your Captain Pappas, and then contact the Chinese Consulate in Rome. Be assured that the authorities will then be waiting for you by the time we return to Athens."

Lin had fought long and hard, but now she felt as though the strength of a thousand suns could not give her the power to combat this couple. Nothing left to say, she fled from them and returned to the harbor shuttle site, knowing she would never be more horribly alone.

GIDEON COULD HOLD OFF no longer. He had given Lin all the time and space to seek her peace that he could.

He hadn't pushed her this morning, had let her cry and keep her worries to herself. No more.

He knew that the spa had closed some minutes before, but he knew with equal certainty that Lin would still be there. And there, he would put an end to this nonsense.

As he marched forward, he noted that both spa pools were empty, with the passengers no doubt reveling outside in the warm sun. Odd how life went on regardless of others' woes. Gideon continued his journey down the hall to Lin's room. The door was closed, and he hesitated an instant before knocking. Still, his worry for her outweighed his concern over interrupting her.

"Lin?" he called as he rapped on the door.

When no one answered, he leaned closer and listened for signs of life from within, but found only silence. Perhaps there was no such thing as a certainty when involved with Lin Wang. He turned and left.

Gideon was back in the dim light of the Jasmine pool area when he saw a slender female figure, head down and hands fisted at her sides, hurrying his way.

"Lin?" he said.

He might as well have been talking to a ghost. Lin didn't look up as she neared. In fact, she didn't even seem to notice him. He was about to step into her path and halt her when he realized that she was crying again. He let her pass by and then fell in step behind her.

As she headed down the hall to her room, Gideon reconsidered his intentions. She had refused to confide in him this morning. What made him think that the passage of a few hours would have changed that?

Nothing, he concluded. He turned away and left Lin to her tears. Though pragmatism had ruled out one option, Gideon remained determined to get to the bottom of her secrets. Feeling no more than the twinge of guilt he'd experienced when contacting Alec, he made his way to the elevator and then below deck, to the place where he was sure he'd find the beginnings of some answers: Lin's cabin.

Among the tools that were provided to the Chief Security Office was a master pass card to all the ship's rooms. Technically, he was supposed to have another member of his staff with him when he used this key, but technicalities might as well be damned since he was using it wrongfully. Gideon slipped the card into the electronic lock, and then stepped inside.

Lin's cabin was much as he'd expected to find it— simple and tidy. No cluttered bulletin board with photos of friends from home... No scattering of clothing lying about...

He walked one circuit of the small space, then went to the folded piece of paper he'd noted on top of the nightstand. He opened it and shook his head upon seeing the neat Chinese characters. He was fluent in several languages; Chinese was not among them.

Gideon was refolding the note, intending to return it to its original spot, when a noise in the hallway distracted him. The note slipped from his hand and fluttered to the carpet. He let it rest, his attention focused on the door. If Lin had returned, he would deal with her head-on. What other choice did he have?

The rattle and clank he'd heard in the hallway passed by Lin's door—a housekeeping or maintenance cart, he assumed. Gideon marginally relaxed, but still knew he'd best get on with his search before she returned.

He bent over to pick up the note from its resting spot by the bed. Something else caught his eye. A small bit of blue plastic appeared to be wedged between the bed and the nightstand.

Ignoring the tug of pain from old injuries, Gideon got down on his knees for a closer look. Shouldering the mattress and bedspread aside, he reached into the crevice where the plastic rested and pulled out his prize.

If somebody had asked him to identify what he'd found by touch, he'd have failed. By sight, it was unmistakable.

"A pacifier?" he said aloud.

Gideon stood and pocketed his find. His was an orderly brain, one with an aversion to unfinished puzzles. He immediately thought back to last week's "stray baby" incident report.

"Maybe not so stray, after all."

So, now what? His duty as a ship's officer was to locate Lin, question her and ultimately report her should she have a baby aboard. The owners of *Alexandra's Dream* had given him shelter when he'd sorely needed one. To shirk his duty now would be inexcusable.

But...*Lin.*

What would move her to bring a child aboard? She wasn't the sort to do anything on a whim. Her behavior since the start of this cruise spoke of a woman in crisis.

It would be a betrayal of his feelings for her if he cornered her and subjected her to more pain. Though he'd never spoken the words, she had to know that he loved her. And though she'd never spoken the words, either, he had to believe that she loved him, too.

One question remained....

Was her love strong enough that she would come to him?

He couldn't give her very long, but he could give her a day or so....

Gideon would wait.

CHAPTER FIFTEEN

A WOMAN COULD NOT hide forever. Or, Lin supposed, in her case, even for a few blissful months.

Tempted by the calm, reflective waters of the Jasmine pool, Lin slipped off her sandals and sat at the pool's edge, letting her feet dangle into the warm water. Was it so wrong to want to stand on one's own? Was that so much to ask of destiny?

She had withstood Wei Chan's death, the arduous months of her lonely pregnancy, and even the constant fear of her child being discovered aboard ship. She had stood fast in the face of Dima Ivanov's threats and had even managed not to shrink from her in-laws' first attempts at coercion.

But just when her goal of reaching Paris had seemed close, Ji and Quio Chan had outmaneuvered her. They could and would see her made a woman with no nation. There would be no waiting them out, no hoping they would simply disappear. They had set forth their battle plan, and she could find no flaw in it.

Lin imagined her life in Jiangsu. She would never be allowed to remarry, would never know the touch of a man or the joy of more children. And if she did something to cross her in-laws, she knew her fate. She would be taken from Wei's life, and perhaps have her own life taken, too.

Ji and Quio Chan had been kind, indeed, in sending off their son. At least he had been allowed to follow his destiny, no matter how dark it had been.

Lin had known from the moment of Wei's death that her destiny was to return to China someday. It seemed her in-laws had stripped her of that right…for now, at least. All their money and their power would not buy them eternal life. When they were gone—and she prayed it was soon, for all the ill they'd done—she would carry on.

But she could no longer fight this battle alone, and she knew of only one man who could help her. That she loved Gideon Dayan only made this harder. And love him she did. In a way, it was good that she'd never given him the words. After tonight, he would never believe her.

BACK IN HER CABIN, Lin carefully prepared for battle. She showered, using scented soap she'd filched from a maid's cart, and then dried her hair and brushed it until it shone like a silken mantle. She put on her bold red dress—the one she'd worn for Gideon once before—and even repaired the jade necklace the best she could, with a bit of thread from a sewing kit.

Next, she called Gideon and asked that he meet her in his cabin. Finally, she reached Zhang and told her to bring Wei to the massage room. When her friend questioned her, she told her that all would be clear before the night had ended. Now, if only her confidence ran more than skin-deep…

She hadn't even made it to the service elevator when Dima Ivanov fell in step beside her.

"Dressed for pleasure, I see."

He frightened her no more. "Not your pleasure, Dima."

"Then it doesn't worry you that I come from another visit with your in-laws? That they think I can persuade you to give up this baby you don't admit you have aboard ship?"

She smiled her best warrior's smile. "Yes, Dima, I have a baby aboard ship, and, no, you don't worry me at all."

"You are not a very smart woman, are you?"

"I am smarter by the minute," she said as she tapped the service elevator's button. "You see, I am about to take your weapon away from you."

The elevator opened, and she stepped in. Dima followed.

"My weapon? What weapon? I carry no weapon!"

She laughed as she pressed the button for twelve— the Helios deck.

"You are not a very smart man, are you?" she asked him.

As the elevator rose, Lin considered her plan. It would lose her Gideon, but at least she had regained her sense of freedom.

The elevator chimed its arrival at the Helios deck, and Lin exited. Dima, of course, followed.

"Come along," she said to him. "I haven't all night."

The service elevator had brought her to the maintenance side of the spa. She walked past the racks of supplies and out into the public area, which was still and quiet.

She could sense Dima fuming behind her. She knew he was about to find his tongue again.

"You think you can push me away so easily? I mean what I say. I will report you."

"But what good will that do you when I have reported myself?" she sweetly asked.

"You would never!"

"Come along if you do not believe me."

She arrived outside her massage room door. She gave the coded knock for what was likely the very last time. The door opened a fraction. Lin went to slip inside by herself and have Dima wait in the hallway. He had other plans. He reached over her and pushed the door open, exposing both Wei and Zhang. She had hoped to keep Zhang out of this, but since the harm had already been done, she mentally adjusted her battle tactics.

"Dima," she said. "You know Zhang, I'm sure. In Zhang's arms is my son." She then held out her arms to Zhang, who delivered Wei into them.

She whispered to her sweet baby in their native tongue how much she had missed him, and how she would fight to her very last breath to see that they would never be apart again. Until he went off to university, of course…

"Why is that ape here?" Zhang asked in their shared language of Huayu.

"I am sorry for that. I hadn't meant for you to be seen, but we will soon be rid of him," Lin replied. In English she said, "And now we shall all go visit Gideon Dayan."

"You are certain of this? Dayan will protect us?" Zhang asked, again in Huayu.

"More certain than I've been of anything in months," Lin replied, for she knew Gideon down to the bottom of his guardian soul.

GIDEON DAYAN OPENED his door to a circus, instead of the woman he'd been anticipating. Lin carried a covered basket, in which he expected was the baby who belonged to the pacifier he'd found. What he hadn't anticipated was Dima Ivanov's presence, or that of another woman he recognized as Zhang Xio, who was in charge of the ship's laundry.

He ushered the group inside and closed his door. Lin set the basket she'd been carrying on his bed, then after folding back a frilly linen covering, lifted out a baby dressed in a light blue one-piece set of pajamas, of sorts. He wasn't well acquainted with baby wear, but he assumed the blue meant that Lin had a son.

"Tell him now," the Russian said to Lin.

She stepped forward. "Gideon, should you have somehow overlooked this, in my arms is my son, Wei. I smuggled him aboard a few months ago, under a shawl I wore." She turned back to Ivanov. "There, now you are weaponless." She let her gaze travel down to the area below his belt. "Though I doubt it was much of a weapon to begin with."

Gideon shook his head. He didn't mind being rele-
gated to the role of spectator in this particular circus.

"Lin, why are these people with you?" he asked.

"Dima is here because he didn't believe that I speak
the truth. Zhang is here only because Dima complicated matters. Both, I think, can go now," she decreed
with a firm nod of her head.

Neither the Russian nor Lin's friend thought to
question her. They departed, leaving him alone with
Lin and her child. Gideon watched as a measure of Lin's
bravado faded. Obviously weary, she sat in one of his
armchairs, with her son resting against her shoulder.

"You must be tired," he said.

She nodded. "Very. Deception takes much energy."

He knew the truth of that. "Would you like to tell me
why you smuggled a child aboard and why you waited
until now to share this with me?"

She sat silent for a moment, perhaps choosing her
words. "I brought Wei on board because we couldn't
stay under Chinese rule, and I had no other way to
find the money to be free. Zhang is a cousin of Wei's
father, and she assured me that this would be safe and
easy. At the worst, I would be caught and thrown
from the ship."

"I'm sure Captain Pappas would wait until the ship
makes port," he said drily. "So why come forward now?
I take it that Ivanov was pressuring you…that he found
out your secret?"

"Yes," she replied. "But he is not the main reason."

"What is, then?"

"My child's grandparents are aboard ship. They know that I lied to obtain Wei's passport and plan to use this information to see that our passports are revoked."

Gideon's mind immediately went to his own grandparents, who had never shown anything but love. "Why would a grandparent do this?"

"They were estranged from their son, and so now want the grandson as a sort of replacement. They have offered me two options—to turn myself and Wei over to their rule, or to have them forcibly take him from me. They are not kind people."

"Ah." He recalled, now, the e-mail from Alec, and he expected that Lin's statement about the Chans was an understatement. Wei Chan's parents must be not only corrupt, but more than a little piggish with the power they wielded.

"I know I'm placing you in a difficult situation, asking for your help, but I don't know what else to do," she said. "I can no longer fight them alone, and if I fail, I'll never be able to pick up my life again."

She was near tears, and while Gideon could face much, he didn't want to face that again. He turned, first, to practical matters.

"Have your in-laws given you any sort of deadline?"

"If I do not have an answer for them by the time we reach port in Corfu, the day after tomorrow, they will talk to Captain Pappas and to the Chinese consulate."

"Time enough to come up with a plan, I think," Gideon said.

"That quickly?"

It was time for a confession of his own. "I already have a friend researching your in-laws."

"*Why?*"

He shrugged. "Habit…instinct…" *Or the fact that I was falling in love with you.*

"You were *spying* on me?"

Gideon couldn't help his smile. "I don't think that now would be the most fitting time to raise that argument, do you? You'd be better off waiting until my inquisitive nature isn't doing you any good."

Lin's glare was warning enough that one day he would hear about it. Gideon turned his mind back to the problem at hand.

"You say that Zhang is Wei Chan's cousin?"

"Yes."

"Did she grow up in the same village?"

"Yes, and she attended university with him, too. I first met her in Beijing some years ago."

Gideon nodded. "Good."

Lin's child began to fuss. She rose and began to walk the room, patting him on the back. "Good, how?"

"All successful warriors know that knowledge is power. Are the Chans aware that Zhang is aboard ship?"

"I believe so," Lin replied.

"Then we need to get word to her not to be in her usual places. I don't want them finding her. And I don't want your son with her, just in case…."

Lin paused in her pacing. "She had been keeping Wei in a stateroom under repair. She can use that tonight."

"And you and Wei will stay here until this is finished," Gideon said.

Her lovely eyes widened. *"Here?"*

"You have before, though not with your son and perhaps not until morning," Gideon pointed out.

"That was different. This is—"

"Necessary." And also intimate enough that it unsettled Gideon. He had desired her from the moment he saw her, but to witness her now, with a child in her arms—that only brought her closer into his heart.

"Yes, I suppose you're right," she said.

"Is there someone you and Zhang trust enough to move some belongings for you?"

"There are two such someones," Lin replied.

LIN QUIETLY OPENED Gideon's door to admit Cambro, who'd arrived with enough of Lin's and Wei's belongings to see them through the next few days. The young Somali wasn't her usual self, wanting to play with Wei and gossip about the day's events. Instead, she slipped out as unobtrusively as she'd arrived. Lin was sure that Gideon's authoritative presence had much to do with that.

She felt uncomfortable as well, but for another reason. This was too intimate…too seductively close to the dreams she'd once held of being part of a real family, safe and warm.

"Someone is overdue for a change," she said to her son. This was true, as much as it was also a distraction for Lin.

She settled him in his basket, then looked around the room. Though Gideon's cabin was substantially larger than her own, the best place to change a baby remained the bed.

"Would you mind if I used your bed?"

"For?" asked Gideon.

"A spot to change Wei's diaper."

Lin smiled as he looked around the room in what she knew was a futile search.

"I'll use a towel under him," she said.

Gideon went into the bathroom and came out with an enormous bath sheet. Lin hid her smile and gave him a thank-you, instead. Then she scooped up Wei and got down to the business at hand. She was surprised when Gideon came to stand by her.

"What have you been doing with…ah…" He waved a hand in the direction of Wei's naked bottom.

"Diapers? I have some cloth ones that Zhang has been kind enough to see to as part of the ship's laundry. When I can afford it, I also buy disposable diapers, for the times when I know I can't rely on Zhang."

"And with those?"

"A ship has countless trash cans," she replied. "And many have seen one of Wei's diapers."

She glanced over to see Gideon's smile.

"I can imagine you shuttling them around," he said.

"I once left one in Helga's wastebasket when she wasn't about."

Gideon laughed. "She must have appreciated that."

"More than she appreciates me, actually." A thought

occurred to her. "What shall I do about work tomorrow? There's no possible way I can watch Wei. Maybe you'd…?"

She watched as something close to terror crossed his face, and she tried not to laugh.

"Call in sick," he said. "I wouldn't know the first thing about…well, about anything having to do with babies."

"You know how they're made," she teased. "And you do seem to like him."

"True, on both counts," Gideon replied. "I like babies. I've just never had much exposure to them."

"Now that he's clean, would you like to hold him?"

Gideon hesitated.

"I promise he's a sturdy child. You can't possibly hurt him."

"It's been a very long time since I held a child, but okay…."

He held out his arms, and Lin hovered close as he settled Wei in his safe embrace. The moment was achingly intimate, and Lin could not help but think about what it would be like to have this man hold another child—their child. Fate, however, had decreed otherwise.

Gideon looked down at her son, then at her. "You created a miracle," he said to Lin.

She could only hope that somehow, he could do the same.

CHAPTER SIXTEEN

THE TIME FOR E-MAILS had passed. Thankful for the advent of satellite communication, Gideon dialed his friend, Alec, first thing the next morning. He was put through almost immediately, instead of having to negotiate the usual hierarchy of aides and assistants. Apparently, his name still carried some weight, and for Lin he would gladly use that leverage.

"Gideon?" Alec said.

He smiled at that ever-so-Oxford accent. Alec hadn't changed a bit. "Yes."

"Damn long time since I've heard from you. How are you holding up?"

"Well," he said, and realized that for the first time in a long while, it wasn't a lie. "It's time to talk out of school, my friend."

Alec hesitated only a beat. "Your Chinese friends, I take it."

"Yes. Have you tripped across anything more about Ji and Quio Chan?"

"Actually, I have. I was going to write to you later today."

"What's the news?"

"Two ugly words, Gideon. Baby trafficking."

"The Chans?"

"From what I've discovered, they once financed an operation out of the Yunnan Province, close to Vietnam's border. The babies were sold to families in the richer, eastern provinces. The Chans provided transportation through a trucking concern they secretly owned."

"You're certain of this?"

"If you're asking for admissible evidence, the answer is no."

"Your gut instinct is that it's true, though?"

That was all that mattered to Gideon. He didn't expect to pursue this on anything but a personal level. If there was even a whisper of truth to it, Lin's in-laws would back off. He was no expert on China. However, even his casual knowledge indicated that Beijing didn't mind a little industrial graft; baby trafficking, however, was looked on much less kindly.

"Yes. The ring was shut down several years ago, and the official owners of the trucking company executed, which is going to make proof hard to come by."

Gideon needed one more thing, something to let the Chans know he wasn't pulling his accusation from thin air. "The trucking company…do you happen to have the name of it?"

"Hang on a sec," Alec said.

Gideon heard the rustle of papers in the background.

"Chaoxiang," Alec said, then chuckled.

"What?"

"Unless I've lost my hold on the language, that means expecting fortune."

Gideon shook his head at the Chans' boldness. Expecting fortune, indeed. He said goodbye to his friend and promised him that they'd find a time to get together soon. First, though, Gideon had a warrior to aid.

WHAT WAS IT about Gideon Dayan that rendered otherwise assertive women passive? Lin frowned at Zhang, who might as well have entered Gideon's cabin on her hands and knees, given the way she declined to make eye contact with him.

"He won't bite," she said to her friend in Huayu.

Zhang glared at her, then answered in the same tongue, "Pardon me for being a little scared. I like my job."

"Just sit down and relax," Lin ordered, again in Huayu.

Zhang took the chair next to Lin's. Gideon stood behind Lin, his hands on the back of her chair. Much as she liked the feeling of him standing behind her, she would have preferred to be able to see his face without craning about.

"Zhang," Gideon said, "I know you speak basic English, since it's required to work on *Alexandra's Dream*. I have some questions to ask you. Can we do that in English?"

Zhang hesitated. "My English is not as good as Lin's. Could she please be translator?"

"Of course," Gideon said.

"What is this about?" Lin asked in Huayu. "Your English is every bit as good as mine."

"Do you truly trust him?" Zhang asked in the same language.

"Yes."

"And love him, I think?"

"Yes," Lin replied impatiently, glancing once over her shoulder. His expression remained impassive, thank heaven. "But can you please just answer his questions directly?"

"Think, Lin. This will give us more freedom in answering."

Lin sighed. "As you wish." She turned to Gideon again. "She is frightened that you will turn her in for her part in helping me hide Wei. She always was the nervous sort," she added, just to get in a gibe at Zhang. Perhaps it was some sort of gallows humor bubbling up inside her, but Lin would embrace it for what it was and hope that it would ease the tension she felt. Yes, she had taken back her power last night, but her destiny remained outside her control.

Gideon nodded. "Assure her that I will not turn her in. The only names the captain hears will be yours and mine."

"Yours?" Lin asked.

"I am ultimately responsible for security on this ship. That you could sneak a baby on board must be addressed."

He was exactly as noble as she'd feared. "But—"

"We'll talk of that later, Lin. Just tell Zhang that she is perfectly safe."

Lin looked at her friend, then gave an incredibly loose translation. "You heard him. Must I be a parrot?"

Zhang smiled and nodded.

Lin looked back at Gideon. "She understands."

"Zhang, Lin says that you are a cousin to the Chan family."

"You are torturing me," Lin said to Zhang. "What shall I respond?"

"You may tell him yes, or you may tell him that he has remarkably beautiful eyes."

"Yes," she said flatly, without even looking back at him.

"That was quite a few words for yes," Gideon pointed out.

"Zhang has a way of running on."

He chuckled. "I see. Ask Zhang if she's aware of Ji Chan ever owning a trucking company. This would have been several years back…prior to 2001."

"So…a trucking company prior to 2001?" Lin asked.

"Ji Chan owned many businesses, but yes, when I worked as a teenager in the battery factory, Ji Chan sometimes hid a truck out back by the waste barrels."

Lin turned a bit to look at Gideon. "Yes. He sometimes hid a truck in back of the battery factory…. Gideon, what is this about?"

"Just stay with me, Lin," he urged. "Ask Zhang if the truck had a name on it, or any identifying markings."

"I have no idea why he cares, but were there markings?"

Zhang shook her head. "It was a long time ago…. There was something…Chaoxiang, maybe?"

"Chaoxiang?" Gideon repeated excitedly.

Lin nodded to him. "Yes." She hoped to heaven that her job was done. She was beginning to feel like a whiplash victim. "What does this mean?" she asked Gideon.

"You're not going to like this part," he said. "Lin, I think that your in-laws were at one point involved in baby trafficking. The truck was part of the scheme."

"Baby trafficking?" Lin and Zhang repeated in unison.

Lin stood, intent on rushing to Wei, where he waited in the vacant stateroom with Awa and Cambro, since Zhang was to be here.

"Relax," Gideon said, then came around the chair to settle his hands on her shoulders. "I have a trusted employee outside the stateroom door. The Chans would have to get through Sean Brady, and I can guarantee that won't happen."

Lin tried to relax, but the fear coursing through her was just too much. "Can't you have Wei brought here?"

"Of course I can," he replied. "But don't worry yourself needlessly. I doubt even the Chans would sell their own grandchild. What we have, though, is the leverage we need to make them see that Wei is best off with you. I don't think that baby traffickers are well treated in China, are they?"

"They die," Zhang said.

Gideon nodded. "Exactly."

Now that she was past her instinctual response, Lin grasped the logic in what he was saying. "But how did you learn about the baby trafficking?"

He grinned. "Once a spy, always a spy."

"I should not be impressed, but I am," Lin said. Then she went up on tiptoe and whispered in his ear, "*Very* impressed."

Despite their audience, he brushed a kiss against her lips. "Now I need to go talk to Captain Pappas, but first I'll contact Brady and have Wei brought back here. And Zhang…thank you."

LOSING THE RESPECT of a man was never an easy thing. For Gideon, losing Nick Pappas's respect was going to be an enormous, though inevitable, blow.

"Thank you for agreeing to meet with me on such short notice," Gideon said.

"I'm always available to my chief of security."

Whoever that next might be, Gideon thought.

"I'm here to tender my resignation," he said. "There has been a breach of security, and I hold myself personally responsible."

"What sort of breach?"

"One of the staff smuggled an infant aboard when she took employment on the ship. He's been here for a number of weeks. I didn't learn of this until just recently."

The captain's look carried all the incredulity Gideon supposed it should. "A baby?"

Gideon nodded. "A baby."

Nick Pappas stood, then walked to the window. Gideon waited patiently for the captain to process this unexpected news. When he turned back to Gideon, he said, "I agree that this is a serious breach, not so much for the fact that there's a baby on board, but because this indicates a flaw in our system. Do you know how the child was smuggled on?"

"Apparently, he was just carried aboard by the mother…secured under a shawl she was wearing. We've been screening staff and crew packages and baggage with the rest, but security was lax in not requiring that she remove the shawl as she passed through. Without giving details of the incident, this morning I reiterated to the security staff that screening of crew must be as rigorous as that of the passengers."

"Very good," Pappas replied. "Now sit and tell me more of this baby."

Gideon settled in an armchair opposite the one the captain had taken, and gave a fairly bare-bones version of Lin's story, omitting everything of the current conflict with her in-laws. There was nothing Captain Pappas could do, and if it came down to an illegality having to be committed to dissuade the Chans, Gideon wanted that on his shoulders alone.

"Where are Ms. Wang and the child now?" Nick Pappas asked.

"In my cabin," Gideon admitted.

The captain's brows rose. "*Your* cabin?"

"Yes, sir."

The captain's gaze drifted to a framed photograph on a nearby end table. Gideon recognized it as one of Helena Stamos, the captain's fiancée.

"I see," said the captain.

Gideon supposed he did.

Pappas rose, and Gideon followed suit.

"At this time, Officer Dayan, I'm going to ask that you reconsider the idea of resigning. There was a breach, and you have addressed it in an appropriate fashion. Other than that one incident, your work has been exemplary. I don't want to lose you from this ship unless it's what you want."

"Thank you, sir," Gideon said. "I'll withdraw the resignation until you might request it."

"Will I have reason to do that?"

"No, sir." *And with luck,* Gideon thought, *I didn't just lie.*

WHEN GIDEON RETURNED to his cabin, he found Lin and Wei snuggled on his bed. Lin, who was humming a melody to her son, looked up and smiled at Gideon.

"I'm beginning to feel hope again," she said. "Thank you for that."

"You're welcome."

For the second time in a very few minutes he hoped that someone's faith in him hadn't been misplaced. Then he recognized the thought as an aftereffect of having lost Rachel, and he supposed that even being able to do that was a mark of progress. His past might be well and truly behind him.

Lin gave him a quizzical look. "Is everything all right?"

"Yes," Gideon said. He sat on the edge of the bed, being careful not to disturb Wei, who was batting his

hands about in the air. "And it will be better yet once
we get tomorrow behind us…. I need you to write a note
to your in-laws."

"Do you have paper and a pen?" Lin asked.

"In the writing desk, over there."

Lin looked where he pointed.

"Please watch Wei," she said, then rose before he'd
even had a chance to form an objection…not that he
would have. Now that he knew Wei wasn't as fragile as
he looked, Gideon was much more relaxed around the
little boy.

"Ready," Lin said from her spot at the small desk.

"Tell your in-laws to take a taxi tomorrow from
Corfu's New Port to Kapodistriou Street, in Corfu
Town. There's a bistro named Siga Siga. You and Wei
will expect to see them there at two o'clock."

She looked up, alarm apparent on her face. "I'm to
take Wei there?"

"Not really," Gideon replied. "Wei will be here with
Zhang and your friends."

"Better," she said as she wrote.

"And I will be there, with you."

"Even better yet." She finished writing.

"Just leave the note there," Gideon said. "I'll have it
delivered tonight."

Lin rose and returned to the bed, settling in next to
Wei. "I'm sure Wei Chan's organization could use you
in Paris. You're quite the planner. And then, as an added
benefit, I could still see you."

Since she'd shown up at his door last night, Gideon

hadn't given a single thought to life beyond tomorrow. Now he did, and something wasn't sitting well at all.

"Lin, what are your intentions for your future?"

"Just as I've told you...I plan to carry on Wei Chan's work."

"From Paris?"

"At first. But now that Ji Chan and Quio Chan will no longer be a problem, I would like to return to Beijing eventually, too."

"And what of your son?"

"I would never do anything to risk his life. He would stay in Paris with others, while I was gone."

"And yet you would risk your life?"

"That is my destiny. For Wei Chan as well as Wei, I need to carry on."

Gideon stood. "Have you ever listened to what you're saying? *Really* listened?"

"Of course I have," she replied. "The words are coming from my mouth, are they not?"

She was beginning to sound offended, but not nearly as offended as Gideon felt.

"I'd prefer to think you're deaf to them, Lin, because what I'm hearing is unthinkable. I am hearing you say that you plan to place your child in the thick of the same atmosphere that killed his father."

"You exaggerate."

He shook his head. "I'm going to tell you now that I have seen patriots killed far from their own homeland by those they fought. Paris is no safer than Beijing should you anger the wrong people. You need to rethink your destiny."

"But destiny isn't something one rethinks."

"Of course it is," he said impatiently. "If it weren't, I'd still be with the Mossad, instead of here, listening to your insanity!"

"Insanity?"

Wei began to whimper, and Lin picked him up from the mattress.

"Yes," Gideon said. "That child you fight so hard to protect is your destiny. You are the only parent he has left. It's your duty to be that parent. Let someone else offer herself up on the altar of social activism, not you!"

"We've had this argument already," Lin said.

"And now that I know of your child, you're even further in the wrong."

"You don't understand duty."

"I understand duty and honor and all those noble attributes. But what I understand most of all is to whom it's owed."

She stood and began to rock Wei, who was crying in earnest, now. "What gives you the right to say these things to me?"

"Love," Gideon shot back. "Love gives me the right." He shook his head. "All these years, people told me that love is blind. No one mentioned that it hasn't the brains of an ass, either. How else could I be in love with a woman as shortsighted as you?"

Lin had stilled. "You love me?"

He shook his head with self-disgust. "Yes, and at the moment I can't say that I'm pleased about it."

Lin held silent for a few minutes, tending to Wei.

Gideon gathered the patience he had lost. Perhaps now, as she saw to that perfect little boy, she'd understand what he'd tried so hard to get through to her.

"If you love me, then you must see that I need to follow my path," she eventually said.

Or she would never understand....

Weary, Gideon shook his head. "I see that you don't recognize your path. And I won't watch you walk down the one you're on."

"What do you mean?"

"I'll help you tomorrow, Lin, but after that, I don't think I have it in me to see you anymore. I watched one woman I loved sacrifice herself. I won't watch another." He went to the writing desk and retrieved the note she'd written. "I'm going to find someplace else to stay tonight. Brady is watching your in-laws, so you and Wei get some rest."

Gideon, on the other hand, knew he wouldn't sleep at all.

CHAPTER SEVENTEEN

LIN WAS QUITE SURE that a wax mannequin of herself would have more energy than she did at that moment. It was as though the cumulative strain of the past several days had emptied her of all that was real, leaving only an anatomically accurate, though soulless, shell.

Gideon's accusations last night had finished off her heart. She'd been restless the night through, and it seemed that her crisis had communicated itself to Wei, for he'd awakened more frequently than usual. Sleep had been a rare commodity. Gideon, who now sat across from her at the outdoor table at the Bistro Siga Siga in Corfu Town, looked no better.

"Shall we go through the plan again?" he asked with the politeness one reserved for a stranger.

Stop! Lin wanted to cry. *Be the man I knew before last night!*

But since she would be begging for the impossible, she simply assured him that she knew what had to be said to the Chans.

"I'll be waiting inside, then," Gideon said, then rose and left.

Exhausted, Lin fought the need to put her head on

the table and close her eyes. Once she was past this day, she could sleep all the way to Athens. As she'd expected, the hotel manager had relieved her of her duties this morning. Helga, who'd been a massage therapist before arthritis had started to bother her hands, was to take over for the rest of the cruise. One of the front desk staff had been tapped to act as receptionist. Lin had only to care for Wei, and to bide her time until Athens.

Tourists and locals passed by, their clothing and languages as wildly diverse as the nations that had ruled Corfu in the past. To occupy herself, Lin took a sip of the small glass of ouzo that she'd ordered with the thought of bolstering any flagging courage. She wrinkled her nose at the taste of the anise-flavored liquor, then dredged an ice cube from her water glass and dropped it in the ouzo, thinking to dilute its taste. The drink immediately clouded, and she found herself more calmed by stirring the odd mixture than she had been by tasting it.

"Good afternoon, Mei Lin."

She looked up from her little diversion to see her in-laws standing at her table.

"Where is the baby?" her mother-in-law immediately asked.

"A friend has taken him to change his diaper. They will be right back. Please sit down."

Her in-laws seated themselves across from her.

"Would you like food?" Lin asked, earning twin expressions of annoyance from Ji and Quio.

"We are here to claim our grandson, and not to eat," Ji snapped. "No games, Mei Lin."

"Fine, then, no games," she agreed. "And because that is what we all wish, I tell you now that Wei is not with me. He is back aboard ship being guarded by the ship's security detail."

If she'd been feeling better, she would have taken fierce pleasure at the red flush of anger that rose up Ji Chan's fleshy face. As it was, she felt quietly satisfied at the sight.

"You lie to us?" her father-in-law cried. "You dare to bring us here and not follow through on your promises? You have been told what we will do."

She glanced at the nearby tables, where people now watched raptly. They might not understand the language, but in any tongue, it was clear that a family drama was unfolding.

"Yes, Ji Chan, you told me what you would do. Now, I think it is time for you to know what I plan to do…. If you threaten me with the loss of my son ever again, I will let it be known where your wealth came from."

He flicked his fingers as though ridding the air of a gnat. "All know, and all who matter are paid handsomely to allow us to license at will."

"I don't speak of your industry concerns. I speak of your Chaoxiang trucking company, and the secret cargo of purchased infants that you carried."

She had to give her father-in-law credit. He bore no outward trace of concern. Her mother-in-law was another matter. She'd jumped enough that the table's glassware rattled.

"Chaoxiang trucking?" Ji repeated. "I have no idea what you speak of."

"I believe you do," Lin replied. "But if you really need your memory jogged, I have a friend here who can help."

She inclined her head toward the bistro's doorway, where Gideon stood in formal uniform, a briefcase in hand. He looked very impressive, even to Lin, who knew that the briefcase was nothing more than a prop.

"That is Officer Gideon Dayan. He is chief of security for *Alexandra's Dream*. But more relevant to you is that he is on leave from his country's secret service, and has many friends at Interpol…friends with very deep contacts within China. Deep enough, actually, that you have been bested at your own game."

"You lie!" Ji cried.

"Do I? If so, how would I know about Chaoxiang trucking?"

"No proof remains that we were associated with that concern," Quio said, and Lin raised a brow at her mother-in-law's tacit admission.

"Ah, but proof always lingers," Lin said. "Like my passport application, something always drifts about in a file, never quite tracked down. Except that in both our cases, it *was* tracked down."

She gave another nod toward Gideon, who nodded back. Both the Chans seemed to deflate a little.

"So, I believe we are at loggerheads," Lin said. "I suppose we could spend the rest of our lives battling for the upper hand, but that sounds very sad to me. What I propose is this—you acknowledge to me that Wei is my son, and that as such, I decide where he lives and how he shall be raised. All I ask is your word. Give me that and I shall honor it."

Her in-laws exchanged a look that Lin could not quite interpret, so she forged on.

"In exchange, I shall acknowledge to you that you are indeed Wei's grandparents, and that if you should wish, you may visit with him…in a supervised setting, of course…wherever Wei and I might settle. This will be the test of whether you consider Wei a prize to be won, or a flesh-and-blood child."

While she waited for one or other of her in-laws to speak, Lin counted the beats of her heart by the blood rushing through her veins. Perhaps she was not a mannequin, after all.

"You are Wei's mother, and as such, you shall raise him where and as you see fit," her father-in-law said in a tight voice.

Lin nodded briskly. "Good. And if you choose, you shall be his esteemed grandparents and are welcome to visit the two of us."

"Yes," Ji Chan said. "We agree."

Lin looked to Gideon and waved him over. "Now," she said to her in-laws, "we may return to the ship. If you wish to meet your grandson, you may do so with Officer Dayan present."

As Gideon approached, his handsome face so serious and proud, her pain at knowing he could never be hers ran swift and deep. She was no mannequin, indeed.

LIN'S IN-LAWS had come and gone hours before, in a meeting with baby Wei that had been cautious and stilted, but still with enough spark of some intangible thing—love, maybe—that Gideon held out hope for the older couple. He held out less hope for himself and Lin.

"Do you think it's possible that we might still be friends?" Lin had earlier asked as she'd fed Wei a bottle.

Gideon had refused. He needed to make a clean break from her. He knew now what he wanted: love, permanence…and a family. In the face of the love he'd professed, Lin had offered him none of this.

He watched now as she prepared to move herself and Wei back to her old quarters. Gideon wanted to ask her to stay…to give him one more night, at least, of the illusion of family, but he would not expose this weakness to her.

"If I've forgotten anything, I'll pick it up in the morning," Lin said.

He pointed toward the nightstand. "Your necklace."

She shook her head. "I cannot keep it. It wouldn't be…" She closed her eyes as though searching for the perfect word. When she'd settled on one, she opened her lids, then said, "It wouldn't be fitting to do so."

He nodded. "I understand."

Lin settled Wei into his reed basket. "That seems to be all, then."

"It does," Gideon agreed.

Still, she lingered. He needed to end this pain.

"Lin, if there's nothing else for you here, then go. I have work to do."

She bowed her head under the blow of his words. "Fine, then. I wish you a good life, Gideon Dayan."

She picked up Wei and was gone.

Gideon wished for himself a very deep bottle of vodka.

SOMEONE, HER GRANDMOTHER, maybe, had once said to Lin that the spirits of the departed spoke most clearly at midnight. Or maybe she had dreamed that....

In any case, unable to sleep, Lin had brought Wei to the quiet solitude of the Jasmine pool. It was midnight and the spa was closed now, its outer doors locked. Even though Lin was no longer an employee, she had taken the service elevator to the spa's back hallway.

She felt her way along the wall just outside the storage area and found the dimmer switch for the pool area. She required some light, but not so much as to draw unwanted attention. Satisfied that she had chosen the proper level, she carried Wei's basket to the pool deck and settled him a few feet from the water's edge. As she had two days ago—*had it really been that short a time in which her whole life had changed?*—she slipped off her sandals and dangled her feet into the water.

Lin closed her eyes and contemplated all she had lost, and all that she had gained.

Lost friends. There had been so many.... Those who had lost their lives in Beijing. Those she had left behind in Hong Kong and elsewhere as she began her harried dash to freedom. And Gideon, of course. He had been

a great friend to her, though he wished to be one
no more.

Lost lovers. Fiery Wei Chan. He had consumed her.
Wei Chan, the passion of her youth…heedless of con-
sequences…heedless of risk. She had wanted to die
with him.

Lin froze. She had never allowed herself to realize
that. *She had truly wanted to die with him.*… She pushed
aside the morbid thought and returned to her contempla-
tion.

Lost lovers. Again, Gideon's face hovered in her
mind. His wit and laughter, too. And Gideon's touch.
The feel of him deep inside her… Yes, she had lost
much.

Lost opportunities. What would she have been, had
she not met Wei Chan? It seemed that the entire course
of her life had altered the day she fell in love with him.
Consumed… Subsumed…

What had she wanted for herself? She could scarcely
remember that girl. She had wanted to teach and to go
back to school, too, so that one day she might be a pro-
fessor. How had all of that fallen by the wayside?

Lost Lin. Had Gideon been correct? *Had* she lost her
path? Behind her, Wei shifted restlessly in his basket. Lin
pulled her feet from the pool, then inched like a caterpil-
lar across the cold tile floor until she could tend to her son.

"Sleep, little warrior," she murmured.

He was a beautiful boy…so like his father, but also
already so much his own person. Now that grief no
longer clouded her eyes, she saw that. Wei settled.

Lin rose and walked to the pool's edge. The light was too low to really catch her reflection, but in her mind's eyes she could see it now more clearly than she had in some time.

Poor, lost Lin.

She had mourned Wei Chan deeply and well. He would live on in her memory and in his son.

How would she live?

With Gideon.

Startled, Lin looked about the room. It almost felt as though the words had been whispered to her.

"With Gideon," she said aloud, and the words bounced back at her from the hard tile.

"With Gideon," she affirmed.

Her path was not Wei Chan's. She could no more live for him than she'd been able to die with him! Grief had blinded her to so very much.

And now she needed to start living for herself....

Lin returned to her son, scooped up his basket and got about that messy business of really living.

Minutes later, too excited to school herself to subtlety, she rapped loudly on Gideon's door.

"Who is it?" a deep voice called from within.

"Lin."

She heard some rattling about, then the door swung open. Gideon wore the same khakis and shirt she'd last seen him in, though both he and his garb were a little more rumpled around the edges. His eyes appeared bloodshot, and his hair had been more orderly earlier.

"What do you want?" he asked.

Her courage briefly waned in the face of his brusqueness. She gripped tighter to the handles of Wei's basket.

"It turns out there is still something for me here," she said.

"What? You want the necklace? I'll get it." He turned away from the door and walked toward the bed.

"The necklace is lovely," she said to his back. "But, truly, I have left something of greater value." Her voice had wavered, but she could hardly have helped it.

Gideon slowly turned to face her. "What, then?"

"My love…"

He said nothing, and his expression remained unreadable to Lin. Had she come to her senses too late?

"My heart…" she offered.

A smile began to grow on his somber face.

"My future…"

He began to walk to her, and joy, pure and sweet, washed through Lin.

"My life," she said.

"Is about to begin now," Gideon promised. He took Wei's basket from her hands and ushered her inside.

Sleep, Mei Lin Wang knew, would come to her that night. But only after she'd been thoroughly loved by the man she refused to live without.

EPILOGUE

Paris, a few weeks later

STOLEN DAYS WITH GIDEON were the best. Even on a day such as this, when the sky wore a somber winter cloak of clouds, Lin's heart danced. She watched as Gideon carried Wei around the small park near the apartment they'd rented, pointing out this and that. He delighted in telling Wei the words for common objects in the many languages that he knew. For her part, Lin would be happy when Wei was old enough to summon up a "Mama"…in any language.

"Come walk with us," Gideon called.

Lin closed the book she'd supposedly been reading—her concentration was thin when Gideon was near—and rose from the park bench. The gray pea gravel gritted under her feet as she walked to her lover and her son.

After much debate, Gideon had decided not to stay aboard *Alexandra's Dream,* which had recently made an Atlantic crossing for the warmer Caribbean climes. He didn't want to be that far away from those he loved. She and Gideon would marry very soon, they both agreed. But not quite yet… Gideon wanted first to see if he could get a permanent job ashore within Liberty Line's home office. And he had his apartment in Tel Aviv to sell, too. Much as he loved his family, he wanted to start afresh with Lin and Wei.

Gideon's laughter—and how she loved hearing that—rang across the open space of the park, when Wei squealed at a pigeon that fluttered from the ground to the sky above. She was sure that one day she and Gideon would have other children together. He doted on Wei, already, and had made passing comments on how much fun it would be for Wei to have siblings.

Lin would miss the friends she made aboard *Alexandra's Dream,* but her days there had been just that: a dream time before regaining the full wakefulness of living. Zhang she knew she would see again. Awa and Cambro, too, for they missed Wei already.

Lin smiled as the sun peeked out from behind the clouds just as she joined Gideon and her son.

"Lovely, isn't it?" she said to Gideon.

"The most beautiful sight ever," he replied. He had not been looking at the sun, but at her.

As quickly as it had appeared, the sun retreated, but Lin knew it would soon be back. She had great faith in the balance of the universe. From her loss had come great happiness, after all.

One's destiny was what one made of it.

* * * * *

MEDITERRANEAN NIGHTS
*Join the glamorous world of cruising with
the guests and crew of* Alexandra's Dream—
*the newest luxury ship to
set sail on the romantic Mediterranean.
The voyage continues in December 2007 with*
A PERFECT MARRIAGE?
by Cindi Myers.

*Katherine Stamos is hoping that a romantic cruise
aboard* Alexandra's Dream *is just the thing to help
her reconnect with her husband. But even aboard
the ship, it's hard to leave the stresses of everyday
life behind, and Katherine begins to wonder
if it's realistic to want their love to be perfect,
when she and Charles are anything but!*

Here's a preview!

THE MOON WAS A SILVER DISK in a blue-black sky, and the waves sparkled with an eerie fluorescence. The scene was wildly romantic, but she was afraid to surrender to it. It would be easy to play the part of lifelong lovers in this setting, but she needed more assurance there was real depth to their emotions—that the warmth she felt toward Charles at this moment wasn't just a product of the setting, but was born of true, mutual feeling.

"Charles, do you love me?" she asked.

His step faltered. He stopped and stared at her. "What kind of a question is that?"

And what kind of an answer is that? "Do you love me?" she repeated.

"Of course I do. You're my wife." He took her hand and they continued walking.

"One doesn't necessarily follow the other," she said.

"In this case it does." She waited for him to elaborate, but he did not. Charles had never been a man to waste words, but tonight she needed more from him. She wanted to know what he was thinking, and why he felt the way he did.

"I don't feel we're as close as we used to be," she said, determined to forge ahead, no matter how painful.

"No one can remain newlyweds forever."

"I'd hoped this trip would be something of a second honeymoon for us," she said. "A chance to reconnect, away from work and the demands of family."

He glanced at her. "And I agreed. Isn't that what we're doing now? I'm enjoying being with you now. I always enjoy being with you."

How could she explain to him that his physical presence wasn't enough? She wanted to feel the emotional connection they had once shared. She squeezed his hand. "I want us to be close again," she said. "To talk about our hopes and dreams. Our feelings."

He frowned. "I'm not interested in psychoanalyzing our marriage."

"I'm not talking about psychoanalysis. I only want us to talk to each other more. To really communicate."

"I thought that was what we were doing right now."

They were talking all right, but she doubted they were communicating. She glared at him, searching for something to say that would get through to him—without resulting in an argument.

He slipped his arm around her and pulled her close. "Let's not overthink this. Let's relax and enjoy ourselves. The rest will come."

She wanted to believe him, to have his faith that things would work themselves out, without any effort on their part. But her confidence in that approach had faded. After all, she'd been waiting for their old closeness to return, to flow back in like the tide.

She wasn't sure waiting was enough anymore. She wanted to *do* something to fix their marriage, but that took Charles's cooperation. Something she wasn't sure he was willing to give.

So where did that leave her but walking arm in arm with a man she loved, but whom she wasn't sure she really knew anymore?